"Excellently written, and as always, I am eager to return to my friends in this series." —Bibliophile Reviews

"I love this series. The characters are people you'd want to know . . . if you could keep up." —KRL News & Reviews

Titles by Sofie Ryan

SCAREDY CAT

A SECOND CHANCE CAT MYSTERY

Sofie Ryan

BERKLEY PRIME CRIME
New York

BERKLEY PRIME CRIME
Published by Berkley
An imprint of Penguin Random House LLC
penguinrandomhouse.com

Copyright © 2023 by Darlene Ryan
Excerpt from *Curiosity Thrilled the Cat* by Sofie Kelly copyright © 2011 by
Penguin Random House LLC
Penguin Random House supports copyright. Copyright fuels creativity, encourages
diverse voices, promotes free speech, and creates a vibrant culture. Thank you for buying
an authorized edition of this book and for complying with copyright laws by not
reproducing, scanning, or distributing any part of it in any form without permission.
You are supporting writers and allowing Penguin Random House to continue to
publish books for every reader.

BERKLEY and the BERKLEY & B colophon are registered trademarks and
BERKLEY PRIME CRIME is a trademark of Penguin Random House LLC.

ISBN: 9780593201992

First Edition: July 2023

Printed in the United States of America
1 3 5 7 9 10 8 6 4 2

SCAREDY CAT

Chapter 1

Elvis had left the building, or to be more specific, our apartment. He headed down the hall toward Rose Jackson's apartment, walking with his usual swagger.

"Don't eat too much and spoil your supper," I called after him.

The only answer I got was a flick of his tail, appropriate since he was a sleek black cat with a long scar across his nose and not the King of Rock and Roll, although he sometimes had the attitude that he was some kind of rock royalty. Elvis was going to spend the afternoon with Rose and act as a taste tester for the treats she was making for Matilda, the little amber-colored corgi that belonged to our next-door neighbor Tom. Matilda had a birthday coming up and Rose believed that every birthday deserved cake or the equivalent, whether you were a person, a cat, or a dog.

Elvis and Matilda weren't exactly friends. They tolerated each other at best, but weren't above teaming up against any creature they perceived to be an interloper in their territory, human or otherwise.

I heard Rose's apartment door open. "You're right on time," she said to Elvis.

"Mrrr," he said. He disappeared inside and Rose poked her head around the doorframe. She was barely five feet tall with short white hair and kind gray eyes. She was one of my grandmother's oldest friends so I'd known her all my life.

"Have fun, sweetie," she said. "I want to hear all about the inside of the Walker house when you get back."

"I will shamelessly peek in every corner," I promised. I was heading out on a spring house tour with my friend Michelle Andrews. The fundraiser was a chance to look inside some of the beautiful old homes in town and support the local animal shelter. I liked to poke around in old places in general and I was always looking for creative ways to reuse and display items at Second Chance, my repurpose store. Michelle had been quick to say yes to joining me on the tour. She was currently house-hunting, but after looking at several places, she'd come to the conclusion that she was going to have to buy a fixer-upper, so she was interested in seeing what had been done in other renovations.

My own house, an 1860s Victorian, had been a fixer-upper. It was located in downtown North Harbor only a few blocks from the waterfront. The houses on the street were a mix of styles and there were lots of tall, leafy trees. It was quiet, but the neighbors were friendly. Something about this part of town had felt like home from the first time I turned down the street.

The house hadn't been kept up by the previous owner, who hadn't even lived in town. The building had looked shabby and neglected but my dad and my brother, Liam, had poked around and concluded the house had good bones. Liam had discovered that the ancient furnace was on its last legs, and the seller had taken several thousand dollars off the purchase price, which made it an even better deal. After a lot of work the house had turned into the home I had hoped it would be.

Elvis and I lived in one of the main floor apartments; Rose had the other one; and my grandmother and her husband, John, lived in the second-floor unit. All of that togetherness hadn't seemed like it should work but it did. Gram and Rose were both easy to get along with. Neither one of them kept their opinions to themselves, but neither one was offended if I didn't take their advice. And they were both excellent cooks. In fact, I had my fingers crossed that Rose would make more than dog and cat treats this afternoon.

I stepped outside into a beautiful, sunny afternoon. The trees were bare but the snow was gone, and the wind that had blown for the past three days and felt as though it had come from somewhere north of Labrador had finally died down. After a long, cold and very snowy winter it looked as though spring might be arriving early.

North Harbor is located on the midcoast of Maine. It stretches from the Atlantic coast in the south up to the Swift Hills in the north. The town was settled by Alexander Swift back in the late 1760s. "Where the hills touch the sea" is how North Harbor has been described for more than two hundred and fifty years. Full-time residents of the town total just over thirteen thousand souls, but that number more than triples between June and September with tourists and summer people.

We have no drive-throughs or fast-food restaurants. Our more relaxed pace of life is what attracts so many tourists, that and the beautiful, historic buildings; quirky little shops; award-winning restaurants and gorgeous scenery.

Michelle pulled up at the curb in her new-to-her car, a dark gray Subaru a couple of years old that she'd bought at a police auction in Bangor. Michelle was a detective for the North Harbor police department. She'd watched the list of vehicles up for auction for months, looking for just the right vehicle for our winters. It had come with a set of knobby, off-road winter tires, reinforced front and back bumpers, and some kind of engine modifications that pretty much meant it would go like stink. I'd been itching to drive the car ever since Michelle had gotten it, but given that I had a bit of a reputation—undeserved as far as I was concerned—for having a lead foot, I was pretty certain she was never going to let me get behind the wheel, even for a sedate drive around my own neighborhood.

"Where's Elvis?" Michelle teased as I slid into the passenger side of the SUV.

Elvis went to work with me every day. He often tagged along if I was having dinner with Rose or my grandmother. When a group of us had gone to the drive-in in Farmington over the summer he'd settled himself in the middle of the front seat of my SUV and actually seemed to watch the movie. Aside from the fact that Elvis was a bit of a backseat driver, the cat was good company. I told people he was Robin to my Batman although I had the feeling that Elvis saw things the other way around.

"Number one, he already had plans," I said as I fastened my seat belt. "And number two, I got the last two tickets Gram had. And lest you think the idea of a cat having a ticket to the show is weird, I should tell you that two years ago I did the house tour with my mom and there was a woman in line who had one of those fluffy little white dogs in her bag. And the dog had its own ticket."

Michelle grinned at me. "And did they let the dog in?" she asked. She was wearing jeans and a deep violet quilted jacket, her auburn hair pulled into a low ponytail.

I gave her the side-eye. "This is the North Harbor Spring House Tour we're talking about. It's been going on for seventy-three years."

She pulled away from the curb. "So yes."

"Like I said. The dog did have a ticket."

The first stop on the house tour was a newly renovated saltbox—the Walker house that Rose was interested in—just three streets east of my neighborhood. The outside was the traditional New England style with gray shingles, white trim and large multipaned windows.

"This is the house Rose wants to know all about," I said to Michelle as we walked along the sidewalk to the front door.

"So why isn't she doing the tour?"

"Because those last two tickets I got from Gram turned out to be the last two tickets, period. And the only house she's interested in is this one." We lined up behind two couples.

"Why this one?" Michelle asked.

"Rose's grandmother was a Walker. There's some family connection to the place."

We ended up not spending very much time inside the Walker house. The interior was very modern—all black and white, cool and austere—a design choice at odds with the traditional exterior. There were no cat food bowls in the kitchen and no fat pillows on the all-white sofa.

"That's not my style at all," Michelle said once we were outside again. "I like things more casual and I need a home with color in it."

I nodded. "The place was too stark for me. And I like things that have stories associated with them, even if I don't know what those stories are. I like to think about who owned the table I'm sitting at and who first chose the dishes I'm eating off of."

Michelle unlocked the car. "That's because you're the kind of person who imagines the characters in a story continue with their lives even though you've gotten to the end of the book."

I smiled at her over the roof of the car. "That's because they do."

As we headed for the next stop on the tour Michelle talked about how difficult house-hunting had turned out to be. "I've been outbid twice and I've discovered there aren't as many small houses for sale as I'd thought."

"Would you consider doing what I did?" I asked.

She shot me a quick sideways glance. "You mean buying a bigger place divided into apartments? Maybe. Could I have your dad and Liam and you to help me work on a house like that?"

"Sure," I said.

Michelle laughed.

"I'm not kidding," I said.

"Your father actually offered his help when he was here last month." Michelle's own father had been dead since we were teenagers and her mother hadn't lived in North Harbor in years.

"You know Dad wouldn't offer if he didn't mean it. I think he's the reason I like old houses so much. And Liam would love to give his opinion on pretty much everything." My brother was a builder who lately had been doing a lot of work on older properties. I held up one finger. "And you have Rose and her merry band of seniors." I held out both hands. "We're your crew. And we always come with cookies."

The second stop on the tour was Gladstone House, a bed-and-breakfast run by Annie Hastings and her granddaughter, Emily. The house had been in their family for close to two hundred years. It was redbrick with red and cream trim, three stories high with tall, narrow windows and a widow's walk.

"You know," I said, "some people believe this house is haunted by the ghost of Emmeline Gladstone, who was killed by her fiancé, Captain Joseph Phillips."

"You don't believe in ghosts, do you?" Michelle asked as we walked around the front sitting room.

I shook my head. "I believe in drafty windows and squeaky floorboards, not restless spirits."

The interior of Gladstone House was much more in keeping with the exterior. The sitting room was furnished with several beautiful old pieces. I recognized that some of the furniture was antique and some of it was reproduction, but all of it seemed to be lovingly taken care of. The end wall of the room was floor-to-ceiling bookshelves.

There was a small table in front of one of the two windows that looked as though it was being used as a desk. The table wasn't an antique but the chair seemed to be.

"What is it with you and chairs?" Michelle asked as I leaned over for a closer look at the one in front of the window. It had beautiful turned spindles on the back.

"They're my favorite piece of furniture," I said, straightening up. "There are so many different styles and so many things you can do with a chair."

She nodded. "Of course. Because you can *sit* on a chair or you can sit *on* a chair."

I made a face at her. "Don't tell me you've never fallen asleep in a chair, or put your lunch on the seat of one or used a chair to reach something on a high shelf or piled clean laundry on one or—"

Michelle held up a hand. "I get the point," she said, laughing.

I spotted another chair across the room, a dark walnut parlor chair upholstered in a gold and cream leaf-and-feather design on a pale blue background. Gladstone House was already shaping up to be my favorite stop on the house tour.

In the dining room there were several vintage maps of the Maine coast in gold leaf frames. That was something we could do at the shop. We always had a bunch of picture frames and I had unearthed a pile of old maps in the contents of a storage locker I'd bought a year ago. They'd been sitting on a shelf ever since. A collection of old glass bottles that were being used as vases was arranged in the middle of the dining room table, which was covered with a starched white tablecloth.

We had even more glass bottles at Second Chance than we did empty picture frames. I was happy to have a couple of new ideas for what to do with both items.

Our customers were people who lived in town as well as tourists visiting the area or just passing through on their way to somewhere else. We had a lot of bus tours stop in. We were on the edge of the downtown, a fifteen-minute-or-so walk from the harbor and close to a highway off-ramp, which made it easy for tourists to find us. Small things like our teacup planters were always very popular with them. I was crossing my fingers that framed maps and repurposed bottles would also catch some people's interest.

Michelle was standing in front of the walnut buffet

hutch on the end wall of the long dining room. I walked over to join her, happy to see one of Second Chance's teacup planters on a nearby window ledge.

"I like this," she said, gesturing at the large piece of furniture. The smoothness of the glass in the hutch doors suggested this piece was likely also a reproduction. Older glass tended to be wavy in places.

"We have a couple of houses to clean out later this month," I said. "I'll keep my eyes open for something like it." We had developed a bit of a sideline at the shop, cleaning out houses for people who had to or wanted to downsize, often seniors. I held up one hand. "And before you say you have nowhere to put a big piece of furniture like that in your apartment, if we find something you like it can stay at the shop until you find a house."

Michelle sighed. "At the rate I'm going that could be this time next year."

"Your house is out there somewhere," I said. "I promise."

"You make it sound like it's a dog and all I have to do is just whistle and it will show up."

I bumped her with my shoulder. "Try to think of it more like a cat. It will show up, but on its own schedule."

Only part of the second floor of the house was open to the public and not everyone was heading upstairs. "Do you want to go up?" Michelle asked, gesturing at the stairs.

I nodded. "I'd love to get a peek at how the bedrooms have been furnished."

We could only get a look at two of the upstairs rooms.

There was a gorgeous maple spool bed in one room with a matching tall dresser. The other bedroom held a cannonball four-poster bed with a flat headboard painted a deep navy blue. It was topped with a yellow and white quilt.

"I'd love a quilt like that," Michelle said as we stepped back into the upper hallway.

"Talk to Jess," I said. Jess had been my college roommate. Now she was a seamstress and part owner of a clothing store right on the harbor front. "She's always buying old quilts. Some of them she repairs and others she . . ." I let the end of the sentence trail off.

The rest of the hall was cordoned off with a velvet rope and a pair of brass-plated stanchions. I glanced up at the stained-glass window, set high up in the wall at the end of the hall. Something in the far end bedroom on the left side caught my eye. I leaned a little to the left for a better look. My stomach flip-flopped.

"Sarah, what is it?" Michelle said.

I pointed toward the half-open doorway. "Is that a foot?"

I was fairly certain I knew the answer.

Michelle leaned over for a better look, then she glanced over her shoulder at me. "Stay here," she said lifting the velvet rope and ducking underneath it. I watched her scan the hallway and check the floor. She was in detective mode. As soon as she reached the bedroom door I slipped under the rope and followed her.

There was a body lying on the hardwood floor. A man, tall and thin, somewhere in his forties if I had to guess. He was partly on his stomach and partly on his right side. Michelle knelt to check his pulse. "I told you to wait," she said.

I bent down beside her. "We can do CPR," I said. "We need to roll him over."

She shook her head.

I didn't want her to say the words. The slackness of the man's mouth and the color of his skin already told me, but a small part of me still hoped.

Michelle said them anyway. "It's too late, Sarah. He's dead."

Chapter 2

"Sarah, do you know this man?" Michelle asked.

I took a deep breath and leaned in for a closer look. The man's eyes were closed and his face was slack. He wasn't anyone I knew. I doubted he lived in North Harbor.

It looked to me like the man had shaved fairly recently. There was no stubble on his cheeks or chin. He had thick salt-and-pepper hair on the longish side but expertly cut. I caught the faint scent of a citrusy aftershave. He was wearing jeans and a quilted navy blue jacket that had a stand-up collar and coffee-colored yoke with a pale blue shirt and brown hiking boots. There was a tiny bit of blood on the front of his shirt. I noticed the quality of the clothing; everything was casual but expensive. I had learned a lot about clothing prowling through thrift stores and flea markets with Jess.

The man's watch, on the other hand, was a battered,

stainless steel, two-tone Seiko. It didn't look expensive. It did look old. There were calluses on his hands that seemed incongruous with his high-end clothing and designer haircut.

I shook my head. "No, I don't know him," I said slowly.

Michelle narrowed her eyes. "But?" she asked. She had picked up on the hesitation in my voice.

"I think . . . I think I've seen him somewhere just recently."

"Where?"

I took another look at the man's face and rubbed the bridge of my nose with two fingers, trying to figure out where I'd seen him before. "Coffee," I said. "I saw him a couple of days ago—Friday—at Glenn McNamara's sandwich shop."

"What was he doing?" she asked.

"He was at a table with a cup of coffee and he was talking to someone on his cell phone. I remember he laughed at something the person he was talking to said. I was getting coffee and I wondered what was so funny. Maybe Glenn will remember the man."

Michelle nodded. "That helps. Thanks." She got to her feet and so did I. "Right now I need you to go downstairs and find someone from the house tour's organizing committee and send them up and come back yourself. I don't need to tell you not to talk to anyone else."

"You don't," I said.

Michelle pulled out her phone. I stepped into the hallway and went back downstairs. I looked around for someone from the organizing committee. On the far side of the dining room I spotted Maud Fitch. She wore a name tag that indicated she was involved with the tour. Maud was a regular customer at the shop. She and her wife ran the Hearthstone Inn, a beautiful 1830s Victorian that overlooked the water at Windspeare Point. I remembered Gram saying that Maud had gotten involved with the tour this year.

I walked over to her, pulled her aside and explained that there was a problem upstairs. "Michelle needs to speak to you," I said.

Maud was a practical person, a former nurse in her midforties who I couldn't imagine panicking no matter what's going on. I followed her back up the steps.

Michelle was standing at the top of the stairs. "Sarah, can you stay here and make sure no one else comes up here, please?"

I nodded.

Maud frowned. "What's going on?" she asked. "Did someone try to steal something?"

"Could you step over here for a minute, please?" Michelle asked, lifting up the velvet rope.

"These rooms aren't part of the tour," Maud said, gesturing at the far end of the hall.

"I know," Michelle said.

I couldn't hear the rest of the conversation but I did catch an exclamation of surprise from Maud, probably when Michelle told her there was a body in one of those off-limits rooms.

I stood guard with a hand on the top of one of the newel-posts, grateful that none of the other people on the tour seemed interested in looking around the second floor.

After that things got very busy. Michelle asked me to move to the bottom of the stairs and continue to keep anyone from going up. She and Maud headed to the kitchen to talk to Annie Hastings. Michelle returned alone just as the first police car arrived. Michelle spoke briefly to the responding officer then she turned to me. "This is Officer Craig. She's going to take over."

I nodded at the officer, who nodded back at me and took my place. She was tall, maybe five-eight or so, long and lean. She was a runner, I realized. I'd seen her at a couple of road races I'd done in the fall.

"No one went upstairs?" Michelle asked.

"No one," I said.

"Did anyone *try* to go up?"

I shook my head. "No." I'd seen several people look over at me, curious about what was going on, while Michelle was talking to Annie Hastings but no one had made an attempt to see anything on the second floor.

"Thanks," she said, giving me an almost imperceptible smile. A second police officer arrived then and she went to speak to him.

After their short conversation the officer stayed by the front door while Michelle moved into the doorway of the front parlor. "May I have everyone's attention please," she called out in a strong, steady voice. Everybody turned to look at her, and several people came forward from the back of the house.

"I'm sorry to tell you that there has been an accident and this part of the tour is now closed." There was a buzz of voices, which Michelle ignored. "Thank you for your understanding." She gestured at the police officer still standing by the door. "Please make sure Officer Cheung has your name and your contact information."

I'd seen Officer Cheung around town. He was about average height with a solid, stocky build and an intimidating stare. Maud came from somewhere then carrying a clipboard. She was pale but composed. The only sign of distress I could see was how tightly she was holding on to that clipboard. It looked like the same one that our names had been checked off on when we'd arrived. Maud spoke to Michelle, who tipped her head in the direction of Officer Cheung. The buzz of voices grew louder.

Michelle joined me at the bottom of the stairs.

"What can I do?" I asked.

"You can head out." She brushed a stray strand of hair off her cheek. "Thank you for standing guard until backup got here."

"It wasn't difficult." I could see that even as she was talking to me her eyes were scanning the people around us.

"Can you get home okay?" she asked, turning her attention back to me.

"I can walk from here. It's not very far."

"Good," she said and then she exhaled softly. "This wasn't how I had planned on spending my Sunday." She gave her head a shake and straightened her shoulders. "I'll talk to you later or in the morning."

"You know where to find me," I said.

She caught the eye of Officer Cheung and pointed at me. "She's good to go."

He nodded. Michelle headed back upstairs.

I walked over to Maud. "Is there anything I could do to help?" I asked. People were already giving their information to Officer Cheung.

"I don't think so, but thank you." She fingered the rose gold necklace she was wearing. The small, oval-shaped pendant had a beaded edge and a star etched in the middle with a tiny diamond centered in it. "I'm glad that you and Detective Andrews were here."

"I wish there was something we could have done."

She shook her head. "Trust me. There wasn't."

I zipped up my coat, wrapped my scarf around my neck—feeling grateful I'd brought it—pulled on my gloves and headed for home. There was already a cluster of police vehicles on the street in front of Gladstone House and I knew more would be coming. My friend Nick would probably be one of them. Nick was an investigator for the medical examiner's office, and when I'd last seen him on Thursday night, I remembered he had said he was on call for part of the weekend.

I couldn't help thinking about the dead man, wondering if he had family or friends here in town. Were there people who would be expecting him to show up somewhere? Was there someone who would wonder why he was late and why he didn't answer their texts? He'd been sitting at a table by the window when I'd seen him in the sandwich shop on Friday. He'd been wearing the same quilted jacket, and he had been smiling as he talked on the phone. Now he was dead.

I felt sad and unsettled; my chest ached even though I didn't know the man. I could see him lying on the floor. I could see his face in my mind and I reminded myself that it hadn't looked pained or troubled. I hoped whatever had happened to him had happened quickly.

Chapter 3

Michelle had said she'd talk to me later today or to-morrow. I knew she'd need a statement from me even though the two of us had been together. I hadn't seen much because there hadn't been much to see. I'd caught a glimpse of the man's foot only because I had been looking at the stained-glass window in the end wall of the hallway. I hadn't noticed any injuries on the man's body. He didn't seem to have a head wound and there was nothing on his hands—no scrapes or bruises—to suggest he'd fought with anyone. The only blood I'd seen was a small bit on his shirt and that could have come from a cut or a nosebleed. It seemed to me that the medical examiner was the best person to figure out what had happened.

It was far less of a concern than who had murdered this man, but I couldn't help feeling terrible for Annie and Emily Hastings. This was their home and their livelihood. I knew very little about Annie and her granddaughter. They were very quiet, private people although I was guessing Rose probably knew them. Because Rose had been a teacher, she knew a lot of people in town. Emily was a bit younger than me, somewhere in her late twenties. It was possible Rose had had her as a student.

Annie Hastings had to be in her midseventies. She had some form of arthritis and walked with a cane and a noticeable limp. Annie was a tiny woman. She barely came up to my shoulder. She had wavy gray hair and hazel eyes. She had been in the shop a couple of times and Elvis had seemed to like her and she him. She was quiet and serious but her whole demeanor had warmed up when she spoke to the cat.

Emily had been in the shop several times as well. I'd also seen her at the Thursday Night Jam down at The Black Bear pub. Emily was warm and outgoing, always laughing with her friends and singing along with the music. She was taller than her grandmother, maybe five-six or so, and they had the same hazel eyes. Emily had to be the seventh or eighth generation of Gladstones to live in the old house. She and Annie had been running the house as a bed-and-breakfast for the past five years. The upkeep had to be a drain on them, but I remembered Gram telling me that Annie said she had been born in that house and she intended to die there, too.

I'd reached my own house by then. I hadn't been born or grown up in it, but I was very attached to it nonetheless. I'd sanded floors, pounded nails and painted walls. I'd literally poured my own blood and sweat and a few tears of frustration into it. I could understand, at least a little, how Annie felt about her home.

I stepped inside the front door and pulled out my keys. Before I could unlock my door, the door to Rose's apartment opened and Rose and Elvis came out into the hall.

"I heard there was an accident at Gladstone House," she said. "Are you all right?"

I nodded. "I'm fine. Who told you?"

"Liz. She had tickets for the tour."

"I didn't see her," I said.

Rose looked down at her blue and yellow flowered apron. She frowned and then brushed her thumb over a spot. "By the time she got to Gladstone House apparently they were turning everyone away. She was concerned that people were going to ask for their money back and the shelter needs every penny that's been raised so far. You know Liz. She tried to reach Isabel but she wasn't answering her phone."

I did know Liz. She was probably Rose's closest friend next to my grandmother. She had a big heart and strong opinions. "Gram's helping at the Fairlane house," I said. "She probably turned her phone off. And I don't think very many people will ask for their money back. They know it's going to a good cause."

Rose frowned at her apron again and scrubbed the same spot she'd rubbed at before with the edge of her thumb. "I did point that out for all the good it did."

I smiled. "Let me guess. She decided the foundation is going to quietly cover any refunds that have to be made, didn't she?"

Rose smiled back at me. "More likely Liz herself, but keep that under your hat."

Liz was Elizabeth Emmerson Kiley French. She

was elegant and imposing and she had zero tolerance for people who had no thought for others. She ran her family's charitable foundation, the Emmerson Foundation, and she was also very generous with her own money, although she tended to keep that kind of thing quiet. She was *not* someone who took no for an answer when she had decided to do something.

Elvis seemed to have tired of the conversation. He came down the hall and meowed at me. Then he turned to look at Rose.

"That's a good idea," she said to him. She shifted her attention to me. "I just made a pot of tea and there are cookies. Why don't you join us?"

"People cookies?" I asked.

"Yes, people cookies," Rose said. "I tried a new recipe, two coconut cookies sandwiched around a strawberry-rhubarb filling. Although I could let you try one of Matilda's treats if you wanted to. They're a good source of protein."

Elvis gave another loud meow. I wasn't sure which cookie his enthusiasm was for. Knowing Rose, probably both. Mr. P. poked his head out of the apartment. He was Rose's gentleman friend. His sleeves were pushed back to his elbows and he was wearing one of Rose's aprons. He'd probably been washing dishes. Rose did not like using a dishwasher. She insisted hand-washing did a better job and no one was going to convince her differently.

"I second Elvis's enthusiasm for the cookies, Sarah," he said. Alfred Peterson was a sweet little old man who favored running shoes and pants worn up under his armpits. He was also extremely smart, quietly funny and scary talented at a computer.

"I wouldn't mind hearing your opinion," Rose added. "I'm wondering if the jam is a bit too tart."

I didn't really want to go sit in my empty apartment. "I think a cookie and a cup of tea is just what I need," I said. "Thank you."

I picked up Elvis and followed Rose inside the apartment. The smell hit me just a step inside the door. "What is that?" I asked, trying and failing not to make a face.

"Chicken livers," she said. "Is it awful? I can't tell. I've been smelling it all afternoon."

I set Elvis on the floor. "Not awful. Just a little . . . pungent."

Rose showed me the pet treats, already cut into squares and packed in a couple of glass mason jars. I guessed the one with the bow was for Matilda. Rose gestured at the other jar. "That one is for Elvis."

"Is there any point in telling you that you're spoiling him?" I said.

Rose tipped her head to one side, a small frown wrinkling her forehead. "No, I don't think there is," she said after a moment's thought.

Elvis leaned forward in my arms and gave a soft mrrr.

Rose reached over and stroked the top of his head. "Thank you for your help," she said.

"Sit down," Mr. P. said to me. "I'll get the tea."

I set Elvis on the floor and hung my jacket on the back of one of the kitchen chairs.

Mr. P. poured three cups of tea. I got a cookie from the blue-and-green-plaid tin on the countertop and took a seat at the table. The cookies were delicious, like everything Rose made. They were crispy on the edges, and soft in the center with a tart bit of jam in the middle.

"These are wonderful," I said. "And no, the jam is not too tart. It's just right."

Mr. P. smiled. "That's what I told Rosie but she said I'm biased."

Rose reached across the table and patted his arm. "That's because you are." When I called Mr. P. her boyfriend Rose would pull a face at me but I didn't know how else to describe them other than they were a couple, and sometimes, just watching them smile at each other made my heart happy.

I sipped my tea. It was hot and strong the way Rose always made it. She was adamant about using a teapot with a cozy to keep it warm and she insisted the tea tasted better when served in a cup with a saucer. Right now she was studying me, I realized.

"There was more than just an accident at Gladstone House," she said. "Someone's dead." The words came out very matter-of-fact, not as a question.

I hesitated then I said, "Yes."

"You found the body."

I cleared my throat before I answered. I wasn't sure how much I should say. "I caught a glimpse of a foot in a room on the second floor that wasn't part of the tour. Michelle went to take a look."

"You didn't know the person," Mr. P. asked with the same matter-of-fact tone Rose had used.

I shook my head. "No, but when I saw the man's face I remembered seeing him at Glenn's on Friday."

Rose turned her cup in a slow circle on its saucer. "Do you know what happened?"

"No," I said. "It didn't look like he had fallen and hit his head. And when I saw him at the sandwich shop he looked just fine although I hadn't really given him more than a cursory glance."

"Maybe a heart attack or a brain hemorrhage," Mr. P. said. "I doubt there was anything you could have done."

"My first thought was that we should start CPR but it was already too late." I let out a breath. "The one thing that bothers me is what was he doing in that room?"

Rose narrowed her gray eyes at me. "What do you mean?" she asked.

I stood up to get more tea. Mr. P.'s cup was also empty. I raised an inquiring eyebrow at him. He nodded. "Please."

"Only part of the upstairs was open for the tour," I said over my shoulder in answer to Rose's question. "They had set up a pair of brass stanchions and a velvet rope to block the hallway to the left at the top of the stairs." I poured the tea and went back to the table, setting Mr. P.'s cup in front of him. "So what was he doing in a room that was off-limits?"

"Probably just looking around. It's human nature to want to go somewhere someone doesn't want us to." Rose took a drink from her cup and then started to get to her feet.

I put a hand on her shoulder. "Sit," I said.

"I can get my own tea."

"So can I," I said. "Sit."

"You're very bossy," she said. She glared at me but I knew she wasn't really annoyed. A hint of a smile pulled at the corners of her mouth.

"I had very bossy role models growing up and it rubbed off on me," I said. I filled Rose's cup and brought it back to the table. I was glad I'd decided to have tea with Rose and Mr. P. and Elvis, who was now sitting on Mr. P.'s lap. I felt lot better than I had when I'd left Gladstone House.

I leaned down and gave Rose a kiss on the cheek. "In case you don't know, I love you," I said. It suddenly felt important to say that.

She smiled. "I love you, too, sweet girl," she said.

I thought about the dead man. I hoped whoever he was, he'd had people to love who'd loved him back.

Chapter 4

Rose was just coming out of her apartment in the morning when Elvis and I came out of ours. She was wearing her gray coat sweater and a blue-striped scarf that I knew she'd knit herself.

"Perfect timing," I said with a smile.

"The key to a happy life," she said, smiling back at me, "along with shoes that don't pinch your feet and a good cup of tea."

Rose worked part-time for me at Second Chance. The rest of her time was spent working at the detective agency, Charlotte's Angels, the Angels for short, which she ran along with Mr. P. and their friend Charlotte Elliot. Charlotte also worked for me. Mr. P. had met all the requirements set out by the state of Maine for becoming a licensed private investigator and Rose had been working as his apprentice ever since. Their office was located in my sunporch. I accepted a nominal rent for the space because they had threatened to move somewhere else if I didn't and I just felt better if I could keep a bit of an eye on them.

The genesis of the Angels was the arrest of their friend Maddie Hamilton for murder. After that, cases just seemed to find them. More often than not they pulled the rest of us into their investigations and I had basically given up trying to fight that. They were good detectives. They were smart and resourceful and not at all intimidated by technology. They knew everyone in the area and they could go pretty much everywhere without anyone questioning what they were doing. As Rose put it, "When you're old, people tend to look right through you." And she wasn't above playing a dotty little old lady if it worked to her advantage.

People tended to underestimate all of them, especially Rose, since she did indeed look like someone's sweet little grandmother. But no one who tangled with her ever underestimated her twice.

Mr. P. was likely the world's oldest computer hacker and there wasn't any piece of information he couldn't find. I'd stopped asked about the legality of his searches in the interest of having some plausible deniability should I ever need it.

Rose and crew had gotten involved in more than one of Michelle's investigations and over time they had found a way to, if not work together, at least work around each other. Rose was pretty good about sharing information with the police although she still needed a nudge from time to time with respect to the timeliness of that sharing.

On the other hand, at least in the beginning, I

thought Rose may have shared a little too much with Nick. As a result, he had done everything he could think of to shut them down. Charlotte was his mother, and like me, he'd known Rose—and Liz—all his life. To Nick, running a detective agency was not something a group of seniors should be doing. And he'd been dense enough to tell Rose that. She had challenged him at every turn and, I suspected, secretly enjoyed it. I knew he worried about all of them, but he also seriously underestimated all of them, including his mother. Over time Nick had developed a grudging respect for the Angels—very grudging—and Rose now considered him part of the team.

Right now the Angels didn't have a case, which was fine by me. I was happy to have nothing more important to think about than what color paint I was going to use on the table I was refinishing.

We climbed into my SUV, Elvis settling himself next to Rose. He liked to be able to watch the road as we drove.

"What do you need done this morning?" Rose asked.

"I want to go through our collection of picture frames," I said. "I think we might be able to frame some of the maps we've ended up with. What do you think of gilt frames instead of black?"

"I like it. It's spring. People are looking for something bright and cheery."

Elvis meowed, seemingly in agreement. Or he might have been drawing my attention to an upcoming stop sign. He was a bit of a backseat driver.

"Could you find that box of old maps?" I asked. "I think it's on a shelf in the workroom."

"It's in the storage area under the stairs," Rose said. "I saw it a couple of days ago. I'll get it out for you."

"Thanks," I said. "I have an idea for those picnic baskets that have been in the workroom for what feels like forever that I'd like to bounce off of you."

Out of the corner of my eye I saw her smile. "Bounce away."

"I've been thinking, what if we outfit them for a romantic couple's picnic? We use real china and wineglasses for two, cloth napkins and a tablecloth. Then we add a bottle of that alcohol-free sparkling wine from that winery in Blue Hill that Mr. P. likes and maybe even a couple of beeswax candles."

Rose was already nodding. "We have some little glass candle holders that we could add. And what would you think about slipping in a copy of Glenn's take-out menu?"

"I like that idea," I said.

"As soon as we get to the shop I'll find you those maps and then I'll see what I can pull out for the baskets," she said. She looked at Elvis. "You can help."

We talked about wineglasses and candles the rest of the way to the store. When we turned into the parking lot a few minutes later I felt as though we had a plan. Rose picked up her tote bag with one hand and Elvis with the other and started for the back door. I really hoped that bag held some of those coconut cookies.

I hurried across the parking lot to unlock the door and then I followed Rose and Elvis through the workroom into the store proper, flipping on the lights as I went. Second Chance was part thrift store, part second-hand shop. We stocked everything from furniture and housewares to guitars and books—most of it from the 1950s through the 1970s. Some items got new lives, like the bench we'd turned into a porch swing or the china cabinet that had been repurposed into a display case for a collector's Marvel action figures.

The store was located in an old redbrick house from the eighteen hundreds, just where Mill Street began to climb uphill. We had a large parking lot and an old garage that we'd turned into a workspace. My grandmother held the mortgage on the building but I was working hard to get it paid off.

As a kid I'd spent every summer in North Harbor with my grandmother. It was where my father had grown up and I felt closer to him when I was here. When my radio job disappeared, I'd come to lick my wounds and stay with Gram for a while. I'd ended up staying for good and opening the shop.

Walking farther into the store, I smelled coffee. Like most mornings Mac was just coming down the stairs, a mug in each hand. He smiled as he handed one to me. "Good morning," he said.

Mac Mackenzie was my right-hand man and more. He was all lean, strong muscle with brown skin, black hair cropped close to his scalp and dark eyes. He wore jeans and a paint-splattered chambray shirt that told me he was going to be doing something involving paint this morning. Mac had been a financial adviser in Boston in his past life. Now he worked at the shop and sailed whenever he could. And after talking about it for a long time, he was finally building a small boat of his own.

The two of us had worked well together from the beginning, but it had taken a long time for him to really trust me, or anyone else for that matter. But over time we came to be good friends, and then, even more than that.

I smiled back at him. "Good morning." Mac knew the way to my heart was a good cup of coffee or even a mediocre one. I wrapped my hands around the pottery mug and took a sip. This was good coffee.

"I put the kettle on to boil and we're getting low on tea bags," Mac said to Rose.

She beamed at him. "Thank you." She patted her bag. "I brought tea bags and cookies." She glanced at me. "You may have to arm-wrestle Sarah for a cookie."

Rose set Elvis down on the bottom step and he headed up the stairs.

Once Rose and Elvis were gone Mac caught my shirt and leaned over to kiss me. We hadn't been a couple that long and we tried to keep things professional at the shop. We might not have ended up together if Rose and the others hadn't gotten frustrated by the glacial pace of our not-really-a-romance and all but thrown the two of us at each other. I was very glad they had.

"Have you heard from Michelle yet?" he asked. Mac had spent Sunday in Portland at a boat show and had gotten back late. I'd told him over the phone about finding the body at Gladstone House.

I took another sip of my coffee and shook my head.

"I expect she'll stop in sometime this morning. What does your day look like?"

"I'm going through all the paint to see what we have and what has dried up. I know there are a few cans that are maybe three-quarters empty and I'd really like to get those used for some smaller projects. What about you?"

I explained about the framed maps I'd seen at Gladstone House. "I'm going to see what we have for frames and put Avery to work on that when she gets here at lunchtime." Avery was Liz's teenage granddaughter. She lived with Liz and was in her last year at a private school that only had half-day classes, so she worked the rest of the day for me. She was quirky and creative and customers really liked her. "And I need to start working on that farmhouse table," I added.

Mac grinned. "You mean your trash-picked diamond in the rough."

I'd found a battered six-foot-long dining table out at the curb on trash day as I was heading in to work a couple of weeks ago. I'd left Rose to stand guard over it and raced to Second Chance to get Mac's truck. I'd managed to get it into the bed of the half-ton and back to the shop. Mac had gotten the table out of the truck and given it and me a very skeptical look when he discovered how battered the finish was on the former.

I narrowed my gaze at him. "You scoff, but you will be eating your words when I'm finished." I headed for the stairs. "And by the way, words will be the only thing you'll be eating because if you arm-wrestle me for a cookie I can promise you are going down." I gave him my best glare and pointed a finger at him. I could hear him laughing all the way up the stairs.

I dropped my things in my office and grabbed an old hoodie I kept there along with a refill on my coffee. Rose was already downstairs with her tea. She'd found the maps and was spreading them on the workbench. We had about ten minutes before it was time to open.

I unearthed the box with the frames, and Rose and I picked out half a dozen that we felt would work with the maps. I set everything to one side for Avery to work on when she arrived at lunchtime. Rose went to open the front door and I pulled on my hoodie and headed out to the old garage space. Mac was coming across the parking lot with a wooden milk crate filled with paint cans.

"I'd like to do gilt picture frames," I said. "Would you leave out any gold paint you find?"

He nodded. "I will. I know there's at least one can with some paint left in it. I'll find it."

My farm table was just inside the garage workspace. Mac was right about the condition of the finish. It was chipped and battered and the top of the pine table was going to need a lot of sanding—it had been gouged in several places—but to me the piece was still beautiful. It had turned legs, a plank top and even a knife drawer on one side. I had a feeling the table was more than a hundred years old and I hated how it had been dumped on garbage day as though its usefulness was over.

I was working with the doors open, sanding the

front of the knife drawer, when Michelle showed up. She knocked on the doorframe and smiled when I looked up.

"You still sort of cross your eyes when you concentrate," she said.

"I'm not crossing my eyes. I'm gazing intently," I said. I got to my feet, pulling off the mask I was wearing.

"Of course you are," she said with a grin.

I made a face at her.

That just made her laugh. "Do you remember how your grandmother used to say your face was going to freeze like that?"

I nodded. "Liz actually said that to me just last week. I told her it hadn't happened yet and she said one of these days it was going to catch up with me." I gestured at the shop. "Could I get you a cup of coffee or tea?"

She shook her head. "No thanks."

I set down the sanding block I was holding. "So where do you want to start?"

"Tell me again how you spotted the body."

"We got to the top of the stairs. You were ahead of me. We took a look in the two bedrooms that were open. I remember seeing the rope and the stanchions and wondering where they came from. I noticed the stained-glass window up high in the end wall and it caught my attention because I think there may have been a similar window in my house at one time."

"Then what happened?" Michelle asked.

"I saw a foot, just out of the corner of my eye. I leaned over to get a better look. Then I showed you."

"Did you see anything else?"

I shook my head. "No. You and I were the only people up on that floor."

"And you didn't know who the man was."

"I didn't. Like I said, I'd seen him at the sandwich shop on Friday but I didn't even exchange a hello. He was at a table and I was buying coffee. Have you figured out who he is yet and what happened?"

Michelle glanced at her watch. It had belonged to her late father and she always wore it. "The autopsy isn't happening until this afternoon so we don't have a cause of death yet," she said. "The man's name is Mark Steele. I'm surprised you haven't heard. The story is already making its way around town. Mr. Steele was the co-host of a TV show, *Night Moves*, which debunks stories about ghosts and hauntings."

"What was he doing at Gladstone House?" Even as I asked the question I had an idea about the answer.

"According to Annie Hastings, Mark Steele wanted to feature Gladstone House on his show because of all the stories about the ghost of Emmeline Gladstone, but Annie had refused to be part of anything like that. She apparently told him that *Night Moves* was tacky and exploitative."

I stuffed my hands in the front pocket of my hoodie. "It seems he didn't take no for an answer."

She shook her head. "No, he didn't. As far as Annie is concerned maybe the house is haunted by the spirit of Emmeline, and maybe it's not. She leaves it up to the people who believe they have seen the ghost to decide for themselves if it's real."

"And Mark Steele wanted to do what? Settle the issue once and for all?"

"It looks that way. It turns out that he managed to spend a night in the house about six weeks ago by using a false name and some kind of a disguise."

"The man was persistent," I said.

"Based on what I've heard, Mark Steele's persistence was what made that show work." She smiled. "And speaking of work, I need to get back to the station."

"There's a house tour coming up in a couple of weeks in Camden," I said. "If I can get tickets are you interested?"

She nodded. "Absolutely."

"Okay. I'll let you know. If you have any more questions"—I held out both hands—"you know where I am."

Michelle patted her jacket pocket. I was guessing it held her phone. "You'll probably hear from Nick sometime today," she said.

"I figured I would."

She smiled again. "I'll talk to you soon. Let me know about the tickets."

I promised I would and she headed to her car.

I put my mask back on and started sanding the bottom edge of the drawer front. I'd been at it maybe five minutes when I spotted Rose coming from the shop. She was carrying a cup of coffee and she was being trailed by Elvis. I got to my feet and pulled my mask down again.

"Elvis and I thought you might like a bit of a

break," she said. "You've been working hard on that table."

I took the cup from her. The cat looked around and it seemed to me he made a face. "And the fact that Michelle just left is a happy coincidence of timing?"

Rose nodded. "It looks like it is," she said. She had something wrapped in a napkin in her other hand. "I almost forgot." She held out the little bundle. "I brought you a cookie as well."

With those guileless gray eyes and sweet smile I could almost believe that she wasn't on a fishing expedition. Almost.

I unwrapped the cookie. It was bait. I was the fish Rose was trying to hook.

I took a bite. Then I had a large sip of my coffee. Rose waited patiently.

"His name is Mark Steele," I said.

Rose nodded. "Yes, I know."

She was always one step ahead of me, and Michelle had said the information was already making its way around town.

"Did you know he's the host of a TV show about haunted houses?" I asked.

"*Night Moves.* I've heard of the show."

I took another sip of my coffee. "What's it like?"

She thought for a moment, tipping her head to one side. "I know that some people have called it exploitative. Of course they ramp things up a bit to make them more dramatic, but basically Mr. Steele and his team expose scammers who are taking advantage of people." She held up a hand before I could say anything. "There's nothing wrong with a good ghost story on a rainy night. It's fun to be scared a little, but I don't like to see people frightened or taken advantage of, so while I think Mark Steele should have taken Annie's no as a no and moved on, I don't think the premise of his show was a bad one necessarily."

"Maybe I'll watch a couple of episodes," I said. Now that I knew about the show I was curious about it.

"I think you should," Rose said. "Did Michelle happen to mention how Mr. Steele died?"

So that's what she had been fishing for. I shook my head. "The autopsy isn't until later. She did say Nick will probably stop by at some point."

Rose smiled. "Send him in for a cookie. I'll let you get back to work."

"I'll tell him," I said.

She leaned down and picked up Elvis and they headed back to the shop.

I was starting to think about lunch when Nick finally showed up. He filled the doorway, pretty much blocking out the sun. Nick Elliot was over six feet tall with the wide shoulders and muscular arms of a football player, although hockey was actually his sport. He was clean-shaven and he'd had a haircut since I'd seen him the previous Thursday night. His sandy hair wasn't falling in his face or curling over his collar anymore. Nick was wearing what I thought of as his work clothes: a blue polo shirt and black pants with lots of pockets.

"Got a minute?" he asked, giving me that little boy smile that worked on pretty much every woman but me.

"I have," I said, taking my mask off altogether this time. "Michelle said you'd probably want to talk to me."

"It's not a big deal," he said. "Just tell me what happened, what you saw, what you did. At this point I'm just looking for background."

Once again I explained noticing the stained-glass window and then catching sight of Mark Steele's foot.

Nick nodded. "Michelle mentioned you had seen him at Glenn's."

I brushed dust from the front of my hoodie. "Friday. I stopped in for coffee."

"So Mr. Steele wasn't trying to be unobtrusive?"

"Not as far as I could see. He was just sitting there at a table by the window. He wasn't wearing sunglasses and a fake mustache if that's what you're asking."

Nick laughed. "I guess I kind of was."

We had an easy familiarity that came from having known each other since we were kids, but for more than a month I'd felt a little awkward around Nick and I'd been struggling not to show it. The day after Valentine's I'd gone out for an early run and seen Nick leaving my friend Jess's place. There wasn't anything romantic between the two. There never had been. Neither one of them had said anything about spending Valentine's Day together. My choices were: ask Jess what was going on, ask Nick, or keep my mouth shut and pretend I hadn't seen him.

I chose the latter.

It was making me crazy.

There was no question that I loved Nick. He was

like a second brother, which made sense in a way because he was Liam's best friend. Aside from a brief crush I'd had when I was fifteen and he was busy trying to go out with every teenage girl in North Harbor and a fifty-mile radius, I had never thought of us as more than good friends.

Nick knew all my secrets and I knew all of his but when he kissed me there was no spark. On the other hand, when Mac kissed me, fireworks went off, bells rang and birds flew over the heather à la *Wuthering Heights*. (Gram may have let me watch too many old movies when I was a kid.)

I stretched one arm up over my head. I was stiff from leaning over the table for so long. "I really only glanced over at the man, you know, the way you do when you're standing in line, but he wasn't acting like someone trying to hide. He seemed fine. And for the record he didn't look sick, either. He wasn't coughing. He didn't look pale."

"Lots of things could have killed him."

"Maybe we'll get some answers after the autopsy."

Nick shrugged. "Maybe. It's scheduled for late this afternoon. But it could be days or weeks before the medical examiner figures out cause of death."

"You saw the little bit of blood on his shirt?"

"I saw it," he said.

"So is it important?"

He straightened up, pushing away from the doorframe where he'd been leaning. "At this point I don't know."

"And if you did know you wouldn't tell me," I finished.

"No, I would not."

I studied him for a moment. "Do you know something about Mark Steele's death that I don't?"

"At this point, I doubt it," he said.

I didn't say anything.

Nick blew out a breath. "Seriously, Sarah, all I know at this point is that Mark Steele is dead, which is what you know."

"Okay," I said. I gestured at the shop. "Rose said to tell you she has cookies."

He smiled. "Let me guess, she thinks she can ply me with cookies and pump me for information."

I smiled back at him. "Clearly this is not your first rodeo."

"Tell Rose I had to get back to the office—which I do. And tell her I know what she's up to." He pulled out his phone, looked at the screen and stuffed it in his pocket again.

"Will you be at the jam Thursday night?" I asked.

Nick nodded. "As far as I know. Save me a seat." He headed for his SUV.

There was something Nick wasn't sharing, which was par for the course. He hadn't once said that there was nothing suspicious about Mark Steele's death. Now I wondered if maybe there was.

Chapter 5

I decided to have lunch before I went back to my sanding. I closed the doors to the old garage and headed for the shop, stopping at the back door to give my hoodie a good shake and brush the sanding dust out of my hair.

Mr. P. was just setting a box of wineglasses on a wooden chair next to the cash desk.

"Thank you, Alfred," Rose said with a smile.

He smiled back at her. "You're very welcome."

"Nick was here," I said. "He had to go back to the office and he said to tell you that he was onto you."

Her smile got a little bigger. She seemed unperturbed. "Sometimes that boy is so cute," she said. A customer had just come in and she left us and walked over to the woman.

I looked at Mr. P. "Why do I get the feeling that she's two steps ahead of the rest of us?"

He patted my arm. "That's probably because she is."

Avery came down the stairs then. She was dressed

all in black: jeans, long-sleeved shirt and Docs, with a wrist full of bracelets including her newest, a woven leather band with a single silver heart charm that she'd made herself.

"Rose says you want me to paint a bunch of picture frames," she said, twisting one of the bracelets around her arm.

I nodded. "I saw a collection of old framed maps yesterday. The frames were about this size"—I held my hands about a foot apart—"for the most part." I explained how all the frames were different styles but they'd all been painted gold.

"We can do that," Avery said. "I like the idea of the gold frames."

"Come take a look at what Rose and I found this morning," I said.

We went out into the workroom. Mac had left two cans of paint on the workbench. Elvis was sitting beside them.

"Hey, dude," Avery said.

The cat meowed a "hello," padded over to her and nudged her hand. She gave the top of his head a little scratch.

I showed her the frames. "These are the ones I'd like to use."

She picked up each one and looked it over, front and back, running her long fingers over the wood, nodding her approval on all but one. "This one has a crack in the corner," she said, holding up the frame. "Do you want to pick another one?"

"You can," I said.

"So which maps do you want to use?" she asked, gesturing at the stack on the workbench.

"That's up to you." Avery was very creative. I knew whichever maps she chose would work in the frames Rose and I had chosen.

"Okay," she said with a shrug. She lifted the top map in the pile and looked at the one underneath. "Nonna says you found a dead man in one of the old houses on that tour."

"That's true."

She looked up at me. "Are you okay?"

I was surprised by the question. "Yes," I said after a moment's thought.

Avery smiled. "Good." She gestured at the shelves on the back wall. "I'll go find another frame." She picked up Elvis. "C'mon, furball," she said.

Rose was at the cash desk with her customer, who had two pillows Jess had made and was now looking in the box of wineglasses. I caught Rose's eye and pointed at the ceiling. She nodded.

Mac was in the staff room getting a cup of coffee. "Hey, how was your morning?" he asked.

"I talked to Michelle and Nick and I got the drawer and one leg sanded on my table."

He smiled. "Very impressive."

"Thank you," I said, giving a little curtsy. "How was your morning?"

"I sold two chairs, two flower vases and I think a customer is going to come back for that sideboard. Cleveland has some metal stools he's bringing by tomorrow, and I went through all the paint."

I put the chicken noodle soup I'd brought in the microwave. "Also very impressive," I said.

He bowed.

I leaned against the counter next to him.

"Do you have any plans for the children's table and chairs you got from Teresa last week?" Mac asked. Teresa Reynard was one of the pickers I bought from regularly. Cleveland was one of the others.

I shook my head. "None. The table legs all need to be tightened and the spindles on all the chairs will have to be glued. Other than that I think it just needs a light sanding and painting. I'm trying to decide if it's worth getting Jess to make chair pads for the seats."

He took a sip of his coffee. "I think I found enough paint to do all four chairs and the table. Do you mind if I go ahead?"

"No." The microwave beeped and I straightened up to check my soup. It needed a little more time. "What color are you going to use?"

"Colors. Plural," he said. "What do you think of a dark blue chair, a lighter blue one, a sage green and a butter yellow? With a light gray table."

"I like it."

He smiled. "Okay. I'm going to get started on gluing those joints."

"I'll be out to do more sanding later," I said. The microwave beeped again.

"Yell if you need me," Mac said.

I took my soup into my office. Elvis was sitting on my desk. "I thought you were helping Avery," I said.

He made a face.

I sat down in my desk chair, still holding the container of soup because I knew Elvis was not above sticking his face in the dish. "Want some chicken?" I asked.

"Mrrr," he said.

I used my spoon to fish out two pieces of chicken and a bit of carrot. I blew on them then set them on my napkin, which I then put on the desk in front of him. He ate some chicken. I ate some soup. "Nick was here," I said. "I think he's holding something back about Mark Steele's death."

"Mrr," the cat said again. He didn't seem surprised or maybe it was complete disinterest I was seeing.

"I wonder if there could be something suspicious about how Mr. Steele died," I said, thinking out loud. I put another piece of chicken in front of Elvis. "I sound like Rose, don't I?"

He lifted his head. His green eyes fixed on me for a long, unblinking moment and then he went back to his chicken. I was pretty certain that was a yes.

I ate the last of my soup and took my dishes to the staff room. I got a cookie from the tin on the counter and went back to my office. Elvis was sitting on my chair now, making a quick pass at his face.

"I'm not dwelling on Mark Steele's death," I said. "At this point it's out of my hands."

I picked Elvis up and he nuzzled my chin. I decided to take that as a vote of support.

When we got downstairs I found Liz in the shop. As always she was beautifully turned out. Her blond hair curled around her face—no gray hairs for her. Her makeup was perfect, helped by two things. She had gorgeous skin to begin with, smooth and unblemished, and her niece owned one of the most popular spas in this part of New England.

Liz was wearing a charcoal and gray coat over a plum-colored dress. Elvis made his way over to Rose while I put my arms around Liz's shoulders and gave her a hug.

"To what do we owe the honor of your company?" I asked.

"I came to see you," she said.

I smiled. "And here I am. What do you need?"

"Channing and I went out to walk around the grounds of the Sunshine Camp Saturday afternoon to see what work needs to be done."

The Sunshine Camp was a summer camp for kids that the Emmerson Foundation ran. Channing was Channing Caulfield, a retired bank manager who had been a financial adviser to the foundation on and off for many years. Now that Liz was running things again she had turned to him for advice. Channing had carried a torch for Liz probably for about as long as he'd known her. I loved to tease her about it.

She pointed a finger at me now. Her nails were painted with matte green polish. "Don't start," she warned.

I played dumb. "Start what? I was just going to ask what you and Uncle Channing found."

Liz shot me a warning look. "What we found was an outbuilding filled to the rafters."

"With what?"

"As far as we could tell, old furniture and appliances."

I frowned at her. "Where did it come from?"

"It seems that Wilson bought new furniture for the cabins and appliances for the kitchen right before he stepped down." She made a dismissive gesture with one hand. "Channing says it looks like some kind of deal with a crony of his. I don't think it was exactly aboveboard."

Wilson was Liz's brother. Sadly, he had turned out to lack both her character and her integrity. She was still straightening out the mess he'd left behind at the foundation when he stepped down.

"We need to find out what's in there and get the space cleared out," Liz continued. "I have plans for the building. I can't even bring in someone to make sure it's structurally sound until it's at least partially emptied."

"You'd like us to clear the place out."

She nodded. "I have no intention of covering up any of my brother's misdeeds, but I'd prefer not to have the family name be the subject of gossip all over town. I'd like this done as quickly and quietly as possible."

I pulled a hand over the back of my neck. "How do you feel about bringing in Cleveland to help?" I asked. I had a feeling we'd need the extra set of hands.

"I have no problem with that," she said.

"We're going to clear out a house for one of Mr. P.'s friends and after that we could start at the camp. Would the end of next week work?"

Her shoulders relaxed just a little. She smiled. "Yes, it would. Thank you."

"I'm going to need to go out and look the space over so I can get an idea of what's involved."

"Jane will set that up for you." Liz caught my hand and gave it a squeeze. "Thank you, sweetie," she said.

"Any time. Have you heard if anyone asked for their money back from the house tour?"

She shook her head. "As far as I know, no. Thank goodness. Have you heard anything about the dead man?"

"Other than his name and the fact that he was some kind of ghost debunker, no."

"So you don't know what killed him?"

I brushed a bit of cat hair off my shirt. "Maybe the ghost of Emmeline Gladstone scared Mr. Steele to death." I wiggled my eyebrows at her.

Liz gave a snort of derision. "There's no such thing as ghosts."

Mr. P. was standing in the middle of the store, acting as a human hanger for Rose as she worked on dressing a sideboard Mac had brought into the store this morning. The old man's arms were out at his sides and Rose had hung two different table runners on each one while she tried a fifth on the long piece of furniture.

Mr. P. was looking at Liz. "Close to one in five Americans believe they've had an encounter with a ghost," he said, "and two in five believe they exist."

"And about ten percent of people think Elvis is still alive," she retorted. "Doesn't mean it's true."

The cat, who was sitting next to Mr. P., leaned around him and narrowed his green eyes at Liz. She glared right back at him. Neither one was intimidated by the other.

"Do you believe in ghosts?" I asked Mr. P. His arms had to be getting tired but they weren't sagging at all.

"I believe that there are lots of things we don't understand yet."

Rose shook her head. "Well, I'm with Liz on this," she said, just a bit self-righteously. "There's no such thing as ghosts. The idea is a bunch of foolishness."

Liz tipped her head to her friend. "Thank you, Rose," she said.

Mr. P. seemed unperturbed.

Liz checked her watch. "I have a meeting to get to."

"I'll call Jane tomorrow," I said.

Liz patted my cheek. "You're very saucy at times but I love you."

"Back at you," I said, blowing her a kiss.

I joined Rose, who had draped a cream cloth along the sideboard.

"The color's too light," she said.

I nodded. "It is." I studied the piece of furniture for a moment. Mac had done a good job of repairing the broken drawers and choosing new knobs and pulls. I didn't think the sideboard needed any "dressing" to attract customers' attention but we weren't trying to appeal to my taste. "I'm not a big fan of sideboard cloths," I said, "but what happened to the woven one with the colored triangles and the fringe?"

Rose thought for a moment. "Didn't we sell it?"

"I don't think so," I said. "I think it's in the closet in the staff room."

"I'll go take a look," Rose said.

I started removing the other runners from Mr. P.'s outstretched arms. He raised an eyebrow at me. "And what about you, Sarah?" he asked. "Do you think ghosts exist?"

"I'm with Liz and Rose. I don't believe in things that go bump in the night unless it's Elvis wandering around the house. I believe in what I can see and hear and touch." I shrugged. "Sorry."

Mr. P. gave his shoulders a shake and smiled. "This is one of those times we're going to have to agree to disagree, it seems."

I took the cloths over to the storage space under the stairs, thinking as I did that I was very glad the Angels weren't involved in any investigation into Mark Steele's death. The whole ghost thing could have been a problem.

I should have realized that I'd pretty much jinxed us all just by having the thought.

Chapter 6

First thing Wednesday morning I was out in the garage working on the farm table. I had sanded the drawer, filled the holes so I could replace the drawer pull with a knob and sanded the legs. Now I was working on the biggest job, scraping the tabletop so I could sand and varnish it. At some time in the table's past it seemed that someone had tried to oil the surface. That had left a gummy residue that reminded me of Gak, the gooey slime from the '90s. The only thing I'd managed to find that would budge the stuff was a plastic bread-dough scraper and lots of arm effort. I figured by the time I was done I was going to have some muscles to show for it.

The sun was shining but the temperature was cool. I had put on an old flannel shirt of Mac's under my hoodie and was working outside, with the table sitting on a paint-spattered tarp I'd spread on the ground. The only part of me that was cold was my hands and Charlotte had promised to bring me out a cup of coffee later.

Mac had just taken the pieces of a metal bed frame into the store. We had spray-painted the side rails because someone had covered them with some rather colorful language—not all of it spelled correctly. The headboard and footboard had just needed a good cleaning like a lot of things that ended up at Second Chance. Sometimes all it took for a second life for a piece of furniture was some elbow grease.

Mac and Charlotte were putting the bed together to show a customer who would be stopping by later. Rose and Mr. P. were together in the Angels' office working on something. I had no idea what—which made me a little nervous.

I had a kink in one shoulder. I stood up and rolled my neck slowly from one side to the other. A car pulled into the parking lot. It had been a quiet week so far—typical for early April and I was happy to see a customer this early. Maybe it was Mac's potential bed customer.

A woman got out of the driver's side of the car. Then to my surprise Jess climbed out of the passenger side. She looked around, spotted me and raised a hand in hello. She was wearing a pair of bell-bottom jeans that were probably older than she was and her favorite caramel-colored, faux suede, fringed jacket. She and the woman started toward me. I wiped my hands on my sweatshirt and walked out to meet them.

"Sarah, hi," Jess said. Was I imagining that she looked a little nervous?

"Hi," I said.

She indicated the woman standing beside her, who was taller than both Jess and me. Jess was five-nine in her stocking feet and the woman, in flat boots, had maybe an inch on her. She had very short hair, bleached so blond it was almost white, and an intense expression. She was dressed all in black. Her clothes were casual but the cut and fabric told me they were expensive. I wondered who she was.

"Sarah, this is my friend Delia Watson. We knew each other in college." Jess cleared her throat. "She's Mark Steele's producer."

It was the last thing I'd expected her to say. I suddenly felt as though my stomach was trying to turn itself inside out. There was only one reason I could come up with for Jess to bring her friend here.

"Mark was murdered," Delia Watson said, flatly. She had a low, husky-edged voice. "Jess says you and your friends can figure out who killed him."

I looked at Jess, who right now seemed more apologetic than anything else. "How did he die?" I asked, wondering where she was getting her information.

"A pneumothorax, after being stabbed with an ice pick," Delia said.

"So basically a collapsed lung."

Delia nodded. "Yes. I'm not going to pretend I understand all the medical details but it seems that air gets into the space between the chest wall and the lung and the pressure from that collapses the lung. Mark had just gotten over a bout of pneumonia, which was probably a factor as well."

I remembered the spot of blood I had seen on his

shirt. Was that where he'd been stabbed? I hadn't noticed a hole in the shirt but I hadn't looked that closely, either.

"I think Rose and Alfred are in the office," I said. "Why don't we go take a look?"

We crossed the parking lot and stepped inside the building. "Give me a moment," I said.

Rose and Mr. P. were in the office looking at something on the computer on the desk in front of them. I stepped inside and closed the door, something that we rarely did.

Mr. P. frowned. "What's going on?" he asked.

"We . . . you have a potential client," I said. I took a breath and let it out slowly. "Mark Steele was murdered."

Mr. P. nodded. "Yes, we know." How did everyone seem to know this but me?

"His producer is here. It turns out she's Jess's friend. I had no idea." I raked my hand back through my hair. "Jess convinced her to hire the Angels. Can you talk to her?"

Rose and Mr. P. exchanged a look. "Of course," he said.

I went out to get Jess and Delia.

Jess put a hand on her friend's arm. "I'll wait out here," she said. "Take your time." As Delia turned, Jess mouthed "Sorry" to me.

I nodded.

I showed Delia into the office and introduced her to Mr. P. and Rose. Mr. P. offered Delia a seat at the long table we generally used for brainstorming—and tea and coffee cake.

"Sarah, would you stay, please?" he asked.

I nodded. "Of course."

"I'm the executive producer of *Night Moves*," Delia began.

"So your job is to watch for fires and put them out, metaphorically speaking," Mr. P. said.

Delia smiled. "That's as good a definition as any. I handle any problems that come up while *Night Moves* is in production. It's my job to keep everything running smoothly and keep everyone happy. It's also part of my job to find stories for each episode."

"You look for hauntings to disprove," Rose said.

Delia nodded. "Mark did most of that. He was very particular about the ghost stories we investigated, but I helped wherever he needed me and I took care of things like getting releases signed for filming. He also bounced ideas off of his co-host, Laurel Prescott." She tapped one finger on the tabletop. Her nails were short with matte black polish. She seemed impatient— or maybe she was just restless.

"Mr. Steele wanted to do an episode on Gladstone House here in North Harbor," Mr. P. said.

"More than just one episode."

"Who first approached the Hastingses?" I asked. I was sitting on the corner of Mr. P.'s desk.

Delia turned to look at me. "Mark. You probably already know Mrs. Hastings turned him down."

"He wasn't dissuaded."

She laughed. "You had to know Mark to understand that he did *not* give up at the first no. Or the second."

"Do you know how he came to hear about Gladstone House?" Mr. P. asked. He wasn't making any notes. He didn't need to. His brain was like a computer. Maybe that's why he was so good with them.

Delia played with a wide gold ring she wore on the middle finger of her left hand. "Someone he knew told him about it. He did a little digging and talked to someone else who had stayed in the house and claimed they'd had an encounter with the ghost. The whole thing piqued Mark's curiosity, especially since the ghost wasn't being used as a selling point for staying there the way we usually see things done."

Mr. P. gave an almost imperceptible nod.

"How did he manage to stay the night at the house and not be recognized by Annie or Emily?" Rose asked.

"You heard about that," Delia said.

Rose didn't say anything. She simply smiled and waited.

"Well, first of all, they never met face-to-face, plus Mark had shaved his beard since the previous season of the show filmed. He wore glasses and put color in his hair. And he didn't exactly get away without being recognized."

"No one was expecting he would show up, so he thought no one would put the pieces together," Rose said.

Delia looked a little embarrassed. "Yes."

"Who recognized him?" I asked.

"Mrs. Hastings. The next morning at breakfast. She insisted he leave right away and she refunded his money. Mark said she was furious."

I didn't blame Annie. I would have felt the same way.

Delia gave an impatient shake of her head. "Mark

knew he had gone too far. He could get a little obsessive sometimes. He called and tried to apologize, but
Mrs. Hastings hung up on him every time. *I* called
and when I told her who I was, she hung up on me as
well. Mark even sent flowers." She held out both
hands, palms up.

"You bought tickets for the house tour under a different name," Mr. P. said.

"My assistant bought them under her name. We
just wanted to talk to Mrs. Hastings. I couldn't think
of anything else to do."

I wanted to say that they could have just taken Annie's no at face value and moved on. I didn't like how
Delia seemed to be trying to justify how they kept
harassing the Hastingses.

"I was supposed to go with Mark," she said. She was
playing with her ring again. "We were going to talk to
Mrs. Hastings and leave, that's all." I noticed how her
gaze slipped down to the table before she had finished
speaking. She wasn't being completely honest.

"So what happened instead?" Rose asked.

"There was an emergency I had to deal with. I was
on the phone and Mark got tired of waiting so he left
without me. When he didn't come back I tried to call
him but it kept going to voice mail. Finally I drove
over to Gladstone House and saw that the police were
there. Someone outside told me what happened."

"Ms. Watson, why do you want to hire us?" Mr. P.
asked.

"Mark was my friend," she said. She looked at each
of us in turn. "We could and did butt heads, and believe me he could be a giant pain, but in the end he

was my friend. I want the person who killed him caught and punished."

"Why not just wait for the police to do their job?" I asked.

Delia leaned forward in her chair. "I have no problem with the police but I can't stay around to protect Mark's interests. I still have a show to run."

"We'll need some time to confer," Mr. P. said.

Delia handed him a business card. "I'll wait to hear from you." She got to her feet. "Jess and I go way back. She says you're very good at what you do."

"We'll be in touch," Mr. P. replied.

Jess was standing by the back door talking to Elvis. She set the cat down. "I'll see you tomorrow night?" she said to me.

I nodded. "Yes."

She smiled and followed Delia out.

I went back in to Rose and Mr. P. "What do you think?" Rose asked.

I sighed and rubbed the space between my eyebrows with two fingers. I had a headache. "I don't know. I get the feeling that Delia cares more about the show than she actually does about Mark Steele being dead."

Mr. P. nodded. "I think you may be right. I'm not sure Ms. Watson was totally forthcoming with us but I'd still like to take the case."

"Why?" I said.

"Because she will hire someone. Please excuse the trendy expression but if we take the job we have at least some control of the narrative." He studied me for a moment. "You don't want to," he said.

"I'm not sure."

We both looked at Rose. "Rosie?" he said.

I expected her to say no. After all she thought all the haunting talk was—in her words—a bunch of foolishness.

"I vote yes," she said. She held up one hand as though she had anticipated I'd have questions. "We both know there's no such thing as ghosts." She looked at Mr. P. "No offense, Alf."

He smiled at her. "None taken, my dear."

"If we take the case, we can make sure it doesn't turn into some ghost story. I don't trust Ms. Watson's motives, either." Rose turned her attention to me. "You don't have to be involved if you don't want to be."

"I know," I said.

"Are you certain?" Mr. P. asked.

Rose nodded. "Yes."

"So we have a new client assuming everyone else is in agreement."

I nodded, trying to ignore the sinking feeling in my stomach. "We have a new client."

Chapter 7

"The first thing we need to do is have a meeting so we're all on the same page," Rose said. We didn't have meetings about all of the Angels' cases. But somehow over time as Rose recruited more people to the "team," we'd begun getting together before any big case began.

"Avery will be here in a little while," I said.

"I need to call Liz and Nicolas," Rose said.

"Nick isn't going to tell you anything."

She gave a half shrug. "Be that as it may, we're having a meeting and he's part of the team." She looked at Mr. P. "Would you please go take the coffee cake out of the freezer?"

He smiled. "Of course."

"Do you need a ride?" I asked.

Rose looked at me like I'd just spouted gibberish. "Why on earth would Alfred need a ride upstairs? Are you feeling all right?"

"I'm fine," I said. "You just asked Mr. P. to take the

coffee cake out of the freezer. What does that have to do with upstairs?"

"The freezer is part of the refrigerator, which is upstairs." She said the words slowly and distinctly as though I were very young or very old or maybe just plain dense.

I held up one hand. "Hang on a minute. Are you saying there's a coffee cake in the staff room upstairs?"

Rose nodded. "Well, of course there is. We can't have a meeting without cake and I don't always have the time to go home and make one so it's important to be prepared." She folded her arms over her chest and cocked her head to one side. "Although I could probably whip up something in Mac's kitchen. What type of mixer does he have?"

I shrugged. "I have no idea."

Rose smiled. "That's all right. I'll ask him myself."

Mr. P. had disappeared, probably to take the coffee cake that I hadn't known was upstairs out of the freezer. I was going to have to check that freezer more often.

I went out to the shop to see that Mac had put the bed frame together and someone—Charlotte probably—had dressed it with a quilt, a striped wool blanket and three pillows Jess had made from an old quilt. A small brown teddy bear wearing a vest that Rose had knitted was perched among the pillows.

"That bed looks so cozy I could lie down and take a nap," I said. "What did you use for a mattress?"

"It's an air mattress I brought from home," Charlotte said.

"Very creative."

She smiled. "I have my moments."

"So did you make the sale?"

Mac nodded. "The customer is coming back later with her husband's truck. I think it was the teddy bear that did it."

Charlotte straightened one edge of the blanket. "I think you're right. She bought the bear and the pillows as well."

"I'll bring in the kids' table and chair set once the bed is gone," Mac said.

"Did you finish painting it yesterday?" I asked.

He nodded. "And I used the last of four cans of paint." He gestured in the general direction of the garage workshop. "I'm going out to start cleaning those metal stools."

I nodded. "I'll be out in a minute."

Charlotte was still eyeing the bed. She leaned forward and tweaked one side of the quilt. It looked fine to me but clearly didn't to her. She straightened up and put an arm around my shoulders. "What's making the frown lines I see on your face?"

I sighed softly. "Rose and Mr. P. are taking on a new client."

Charlotte raised an eyebrow. "We didn't take a vote. And more importantly, we didn't have tea and cake so I don't think it's binding." She smiled. She was a bit taller than me with the posture and measured gaze of the teacher and high school principal she had once been. I could always count on Charlotte to be the voice of reason.

I leaned my head against hers. "All of that will be happening at lunchtime. And yes there will be cake.

Apparently Rose keeps a backup one in the staff room refrigerator."

"Who is the provisional client?" Charlotte asked.

"Her name is Delia Watson. She is Mark Steele's producer."

"The man who died."

"Yes. She wants to find out who killed him and she wants someone to be, I guess you'd call it an advocate for him." I straightened up.

"And there's something about this woman you don't like."

Charlotte didn't miss much.

"Let's just say I don't totally trust her motives. You know that Mr. Steele tried multiple times to get Annie Hastings to agree to be part of his TV show?"

Charlotte gave her head a little shake. "He didn't seem to grasp the concept of no meaning no."

I pulled a hand back through my hair. "Delia Watson was party to all of that. And when she spoke about the show she spoke about it as if it's going to continue without Mr. Steele. She mentioned he had a co-host. I don't want to see what happened to him end up being used as a way to exploit the Hastingses or anyone else in town."

"I feel bad for Annie," Charlotte said.

"Do you know her?" I asked.

"Yes, but not well. We were in school together but I wouldn't say we were ever really friends. Annie always was a quiet, private person but she became even more so in the last few years since her arthritis got so bad." She eyed the bed again then reached over and adjusted one of the pillows. She finally seemed satisfied with it. When the customer came back it was all going to be taken apart again, but I knew if I pointed that out Charlotte would say that didn't mean it shouldn't look nice now.

"Sarah, have you seen the show?" she asked.

"No," I said. "Have you?"

She nodded. "Yes. I've watched a couple of episodes with a friend."

I gave her a knowing smile and bumped her with my hip. "Does this friend have a name?" Charlotte had been seeing someone but was keeping the relationship very quiet.

"Yes, he has a name," she retorted, "and it's none of your concern."

"Well, at least now I know the mystery man likes *Night Moves*. It's a start. How many men in your age bracket in this town watch the show?"

"Who says he's in my age bracket?" Charlotte countered.

I put my hands on my hips and eyed her in surprise. "Charlotte Elliot, I am learning there are sides to you I've never seen before."

She gave me a saucy smile. "You are only scratching the surface."

I laughed all the way out to the workshop.

I worked on the table for the rest of the morning, making progress, albeit very slowly. Mac got us each a cup of coffee at one point and we each looked over the other's project.

"What are your plans for the stools?" I asked, walking around the four of them so I could check them out from every angle.

"Clean them, obviously. There's something sticky on the legs. I think I can get the dents out of the seats of those three." He pointed at the first three stools in the row.

"Cleveland said he tried the plunger trick but it didn't work," I said.

"I know," Mac said. "I have another idea."

I turned around to look at him. "Am I going to like it?"

"You will if it works. I'm going to use a hair dryer or something to warm the top of the stool and then push the dent up from the underside."

"Isn't that the kind of idea that usually comes with the caveat, don't try this at home?"

"So you don't think it will work?"

I pushed on one of the stools. The dent wasn't that big, but it looked pretty permanent to me. It wasn't the same as getting a dent out of a soda bottle. "I will concede it might work but please be careful. Those stools will get very hot very quickly."

"I promise to be safe," he said.

"It looks like the Angels have a case," I said, coming to stand next to him.

"Mark Steele."

"Yes. His producer, a woman named Delia Watson, knew Jess when they were in college."

"So the producer is the client? What about Steele's family?"

"I don't think he had any. Delia didn't mention a

spouse or children. I think his whole life was his work."

Mac shook his head. "That used to be me. I'm glad it's not me anymore."

I smiled. "I almost forgot, Rose is getting the band together for a vote at lunchtime."

He reached over and picked a clump of cat hair from my sleeve. "Will there be cake?" he asked.

"Charlotte said the vote isn't binding without one and it turns out Rose keeps an emergency cake in the staff room freezer."

"Good to know."

"Rose also wants to know what you have for a mixer."

Mac suddenly looked uncertain. "Do I want to know why?"

I grinned. "I'm thinking no."

He pulled me against him for a moment and kissed the top of my head. "Are we still going out to the Sunshine Camp this afternoon?"

I pulled away and stood in front of him, stuffing my hands in my pockets. "Yes. I've decided I'm not getting involved in this case and I made a promise to Liz."

Mac's dark eyes narrowed. "Why don't you want to be involved?"

"I don't trust Delia Watson. I don't have any basis for feeling that way. Something about her just didn't sit right." I sounded a little defensive, I realized.

"Hey, I'm not doubting your instincts but Mr. P. has pretty good ones as well. I take it he didn't agree with you?"

"He does think Delia is hiding something as well, he just believes that if the Angels take the case they can find who killed Mark Steele and make sure his show doesn't exploit anyone."

Mac shrugged. "If anyone can do that it's Rose, Mr. P. and their crew."

I slid an elastic off my arm and pulled my hair back into a ponytail. "You are right about that. People do tend to underestimate them."

Jess called just before lunch. "I'm sorry I ambushed you like that," she said. "I would have called, but Delia was with me the whole time. I was gobsmacked when she walked in this morning. I haven't seen or spoken to her in at least ten years." Jess had been binge-watching *The Great British Baking Show* and the odd British expression kept turning up in her speech. "She was talking about bringing in some investigator that she'd used on the show and I couldn't see how that would be good. Rose and Alfred seemed like a lot better option. I hope that doesn't make me one of those small-town snobs."

"You're not a small-town snob," I said. "I admit *I* was a little gobsmacked when you two showed up but I do agree that the Angels are a better choice than some stranger. And Rose and her merry band are good at what they do."

"I take it Delia is going to get an official yes shortly."

"It looks that way."

"If Nick's head explodes promise me you'll take photos."

Here was a chance to ask her what—if anything—was going on with him. And I chickened out.

Again.

"Nick is part of the team now," I reminded her.

She gave a snort of laughter. "More like he's infiltrated the team to find out what Rose is up to." I heard someone else's voice in the background. "I have to go," Jess said. "I'll see you tomorrow night."

"I'll be there," I promised. We said good-bye and ended the call.

Avery arrived about fifteen minutes later. "We're having a meeting," I said. "I'll need you to handle customers for a while."

"Yeah, I know," she said. "Rose texted me. You want me to work on the web orders between customers?"

"Yes please." I waved a hand in the direction of the Angels' office. "There's cake. Get yourself a piece before we start."

I went up to my own office to change my shirt and when I came back down Liz had arrived. "Why couldn't I have given my proxy to someone?" she asked.

"It doesn't work that way," Rose said firmly.

"Well, it should," Liz retorted.

"Well, it doesn't."

I could see where this was going. I stepped between them. "Mac and I are going out to the camp this afternoon," I said.

"Rose and I are having a conversation about meeting protocols," Liz said. "You're interrupting."

"No. You and Rose are playing a game of did-too–did-not. What's going on?"

For a moment Liz said nothing then she sighed. "Just when I think we've found all the boneheaded things Wilson did, I unearth another."

"I'm sorry," I said.

"Talk to me about this new client," Liz said. "Where do you stand?"

"I'm trying to be neutral."

"In other words you're a no vote."

"I didn't say that."

Liz rolled her eyes. "Your head is like a big glass fishbowl. I can see what you're thinking."

I made a face at her. "Fine. Rose and Mr. P. want to take on the client and I am less enthusiastic, but I don't want them to turn the case down because of me so I'm trying to stay neutral."

Liz leaned toward me. "We could stage a coup if you want to."

"Thank you, but no. I don't want to see the Hastingses or North Harbor made fun of on a TV show. Rose and Alfred won't let that happen."

"So your vote is not as much of a no as you said."

I looked at Liz for a long moment. "I see what you did," I finally said.

Liz patted my cheek. "Good to know getting dropped on your head as a baby didn't cause any lasting damage."

To my surprise Nick showed up right before we started. He came and stood next to me. "What are you doing here?" I asked. He was wearing a gray sweater and black pants with a black wool coat. He smelled like Hugo aftershave.

"Rose said there was a team meeting and somehow I seem to be part of the team whether I want to be or not. Plus this way at least I know what's going on."

I elbowed him. "And there's cake."

He nodded. "And there's cake."

I handed him a plate. I had coffee. I leaned over and swiped a bite of the cake for myself.

Nick tried to jab me with his fork but missed.

I smirked at him.

Mr. P. called the meeting to order. He explained the Angels had a potential client. "Her name is Delia Watson. She was . . . is the late Mark Steele's producer and she wants to hire us to figure out who killed him."

"Do you trust her?" Liz asked.

"Not completely," Rose answered, "but if we take the case we can figure out what she might be up to."

"So you two are both yes?"

Mr. P. nodded.

"So am I," Liz said, raising her teacup.

"Both Emily and her father were my students," Charlotte said. "I'm in."

Rose looked at me.

"I have reservations but I vote yes, too," I said.

Mr. P. raised his eyebrows but didn't say anything.

"Mac is a yes," Rose said.

"Mac isn't here," Liz immediately said.

"He's with a customer. He already gave me his yes," Rose said with an edge of impatience.

"So in other words you have his proxy."

Rose's gray eyes narrowed. Liz seemed determined

to poke the tiger. "No," Rose said. "Mac took part in early voting." She turned to look at Nick, whose mouth was full of cake.

I grabbed the hand holding his fork, waved it in the air and said, "Nick votes yes as well."

Rose clapped her hands together. "So we're agreed."

Mr. P. caught my eye, smiled and mouthed the words *unus pro omnibus.*

"*Omnes pro uno,*" I said softly.

If the Angels had a motto this was it: One for all, all for one.

Chapter 8

Nick took the mug out of my hand and drank the last of my coffee. I swatted his hand and snatched it back. He grinned. "That's payback for voting on my behalf when my mouth was full."

I made a face at him. "Number one, don't stuff so much cake in your mouth and then you can speak for yourself. And number two, if you want to change your vote go tell Rose."

He glanced in Rose's direction. "No, I'm good." He pushed away from the wall.

"Are you coming tomorrow night?" I asked.

"I am," he said. "It's your turn to buy the chips and salsa."

I grinned. "So don't be late or Jess will have eaten everything."

Nick went to speak to Mr. P. I walked over to Liz. "So I'll talk to you tonight," I said.

She pulled on her gloves. "The sooner I can get that mess dealt with the better."

I gave her a quick, sideways hug.

"I'm going to help Mac and Avery in the shop," Charlotte said, "so I'll walk out with Liz."

I nodded. "Okay. I'll be there in a couple of minutes."

Nick was on his way out as well. He looked back in my direction. I raised a hand in good-bye and he did the same. I joined Rose and Mr. P.

"Where are you going to start?" I asked. It occurred to me that aside from the bite I'd swiped from Nick's plate, I hadn't actually had any cake.

"Since this all began with Mark Steele's interest in Gladstone House I think we should start there," Mr. P. said. "I'm going to the library to dig into the archives."

"I can drive you," I said.

He smiled. "Thank you, but it's a nice day and I'd like to walk."

"And I'm going to watch a couple of episodes of *Night Moves* and try to get a better sense of what the show is like," Rose said. "Charlotte will see what she can learn about the Gladstone family." She reached over and brushed a stray strand of hair off my face. "I meant what I said, you know. You don't have to be involved."

"I know," I said. "We look out for each other. I'm as involved as you need me to be."

Mr. P. left for the library, messenger bag across his body. Rose settled at his desk wearing a pair of oversize headphones to watch *Night Moves*. Avery was at the workbench packing the website orders with help from Elvis, which mostly meant he poked his head into every box.

Mac was on his way outside. "Five minutes?" he asked as he passed me.

I nodded. "I just need to tell Charlotte we're leaving and get my jacket."

Charlotte was standing in the middle of the shop, hands on her hips, looking at a wooden rocking chair. It had been in and out of the shop proper for several months and never seemed to sell. She looked over her shoulder at me. "We need more bears," she said.

"Not a sentence you hear that often," I said, joining her.

She smiled. "I'm determined to find this chair a new home. I thought some pillows and a teddy bear might make it look more inviting."

"Tried it," I said. "One pillow and one teddy bear. Two pillows and one teddy bear. One pillow and two teddy bears."

Charlotte squinted at the chair. "What about a couple of pillows and a throw?"

"Tried that, too. And seat pads."

"What if I just stuck a sign on the back that says, 'Please Buy Me'?"

I grinned at her. "That I haven't tried."

She smiled.

"Mac and I are leaving now," I said.

"Avery and I can hold down the fort and Rose is here if we need help." She tucked her hands in the front pockets of her blue denim apron. "Thank you for taking on this project."

"I would do anything for Liz."

"More than once I've had the urge to coldcock Wilson with my soup pot for the grief he's caused Liz."

I leaned sideways and rested my head against hers for a moment. "Remind me never to get on your bad side," I said.

We took Mac's truck out to the Sunshine Camp. It was located just outside of North Harbor close to Swift Hills Park.

"You look as though you're thinking deep thoughts," Mac said. We'd been on the road for about ten minutes.

"Do you believe in ghosts?" I asked. "Mr. P. does."

"That doesn't surprise me."

I turned to look at him. "Seriously? It surprised the heck out of me."

He shrugged. "C'mon, you know Alfred. He's very open-minded."

"But he believes in logic and the scientific method."

"Those beliefs don't cancel out all the others."

"You didn't answer my question," I said, shifting in my seat a little. "Do you believe in ghosts?"

He took a moment before he answered, eyes fixed on the road. "I can't give you a yes or no answer to that question. It's more complicated than that."

"Complicated how?"

He glanced over at me. "What do you think happens when we die?"

"I don't know. I don't really believe in the traditional definitions of heaven and hell. I don't know if there's an afterlife and I'll get to see my dad when I die, but a tiny part of me hopes it's a possibility. I want to believe that some part of him lives on in some way."

"You know my grandfather died when I was a teenager."

I nodded. Mac had told me that he and his grandfather had been close. He was the one who had first taken Mac sailing. But Mac rarely talked about the man and I had never liked to push.

"Gramps was a drop-dead practical man," he said, a smile playing across his face. "He believed when we died that was the end. He liked to say dead is dead. He told my mother that we should put his body out in the garden as fertilizer for his pumpkins. She didn't see the humor in that, by the way. But we were out on the water one day and he told me that just in case he was wrong about there being an afterlife, if he found out there was, he would leave me a sign. Those were his exact words: 'I'll leave you a sign.'"

"What happened?" I asked. Was Mac going to tell me that he'd seen his grandfather's ghost?

"He sent me a sign."

I frowned. "He sent you a sign. What was it?"

He smiled. "A sign, Sarah. A yellow metal 'Yield' sign to be exact. The morning of my grandfather's funeral it was lying at the end of the dock at his house."

He held up one hand. "And before you say anything, yes I know there are all sorts of logical explanations for how that sign might have gotten there. And one of them is most likely what happened. On the other hand, though, he did say he would leave me a sign and that's exactly the kind of thing he would have done when he was alive." He glanced at me again. "So do I believe in ghosts? I don't know that there's any incontrovertible evidence that ghosts are real but I don't know of any unassailable evidence that they aren't, either. I guess you could say I'm looking for another sign?"

I stared at him for so long without speaking that finally he said, "Did I say something wrong?"

I shook my head. "No. I was just thinking that I have never met anyone as open-minded as you are. And if there is an afterlife, just some never-ending sea of energy when we die, or even the opportunity to be reincarnated as a left-handed, short reliever for the Red Sox, if you won't be there, I'm not going."

He caught my hand and gave it a squeeze. Then he lifted it to his mouth and kissed my palm. "I don't plan on being anywhere you're not, in this life and however many others that come after it."

I had the key to unlock the camp gate. We parked in front of the main building.

Mac turned in a slow circle taking in the trees towering overhead, the blue sky and nothing but the sound of the birds. "This place is incredible," he said.

I pointed to the trail that ran behind the main building. "There's a stream back there that feeds into a pond where the kids swim and canoe. When I was a kid we came out here a few times to skate."

"Did you ever come here as a camper?" Mac asked.

I shook my head. "Never. The camp was intended from the beginning as a place for kids who wouldn't otherwise get to have the experience. That was Liz's influence on her grandfather."

We started walking to the building Liz wanted us to clean out. It was just one story, longer than it was wide with a veranda that stretched across the front.

"Do you know what this building used to be?" Mac asked.

"I think it was some sort of arts and crafts center but Liz wants to turn it into clinic space so they can accommodate more kids with special needs."

He nodded. "That veranda could easily be modified."

There were some kind of faded green roller blinds on the windows on either side of the door so we couldn't see inside. The lock was stiff and the key wouldn't make more than a quarter turn. I pulled it out and tried again but I couldn't get it to work.

"Let me try," Mac said.

I handed over the key.

He wiggled it a little in the lock and it turned smoothly and easily.

"How did you do that?" I asked.

He handed the key back to me and I slipped it into my jeans pocket. "I'm sure you loosened it for me," he said, raising an eyebrow.

"Good answer," I said, bumping his shoulder with mine.

The inside of the building was worse than I'd expected. It looked as though things had just been shoved inside haphazardly. Furniture was piled on top of more furniture as though a giant toddler had picked up a handful of toys and dropped them. It wasn't possible to get more than five feet beyond the doorway.

"Do you smell that?" Mac asked. There were four chairs piled on top of one another right in front of us and I didn't know if I could remove any one of them without the others falling on me.

I nodded. "That's mold."

"At the very least."

There were several old stoves and a refrigerator in the space as well as a pile of bed frames, numerous mattresses, dressers and nightstands, and chairs that looked like they came from a dentist's waiting room, not a camp bunk room.

I blew out a breath. "This is a big job. We're going to need gloves and respirators and we're definitely going to need Cleveland. Maybe Memphis as well." Memphis was Cleveland's younger brother. Among other things he was a whiz with electronics.

Mac nodded. "With a couple of good dollies and some kind of a makeshift ramp, Cleveland and I can move the appliances."

I lifted a chair off the top of a dresser that was lying on its side and managed to squeeze into the small space behind it. I was very aware that the piles of furniture all around me could topple at any time. "Some of the furniture may be salvageable," I said. "The dressers look like they're solid wood. I'm guessing the bed frames are as well. We're going to need a big trailer or a truck."

"Cleveland has a couple of trailers we could probably use," Mac said. He was trying to find a way around two bed frames that were standing on their ends with three nightstands piled one on top of the other in between them.

I pulled myself back up onto the overturned dresser and jumped down to the other side. My jeans were covered in dust. "I've seen all I need to see," I said.

We stepped back out onto the veranda and I locked the door.

Mac leaned against the railing of the stairs while I brushed some of the dust from my pants. "What do you think?" he said.

I blew out a frustrated breath and straightened up. "I think that most if not all of that furniture didn't come from this camp and there's no way those appliances did. I don't have a clue what Wilson was up to but I think he was running some kind of scam."

He nodded. "I don't think any of those chairs belonged here. They look like the seats in my dentist's waiting room."

"I thought the same thing," I said. "I'm going to suggest to Liz that she gets Channing to go over the camp's finances in detail before we move anything. This is just odd. I don't want to take a single piece of furniture out of this building until we have a better idea how it ended up here in the first place."

Mr. P. returned from the library just after Mac and I got back. He drove home with Rose and me at the end of the day.

"Do you have supper plans?" Rose asked as we pulled out of the parking lot.

"I'm thinking French toast, the last piece of turkey bacon and some fried tomatoes as a vegetable," I said. Since Rose taught me to cook I'd gotten more adventurous in the kitchen. Mr. P. had loaned me his bread machine and I'd made a pretty good loaf of granola bread. I had a feeling the bread would make great French toast.

"Why don't you join Alfred and me for supper?" Rose said. "It's nothing fancy, just spaghetti." Rose made fantastic spaghetti sauce with lots of vegetables and served freshly grated parmesan on top.

"Please do," Mr. P. said.

"Merow!" Elvis said from the backseat.

"Are you sure I'm not interrupting a romantic dinner?" I asked. Mac was working on his boat tonight. He'd come to North Harbor originally to get more experience sailing with the goal of eventually building his own small wooden boat. He had done lots of sailing but work and life and some crime-solving seniors had taken up all of his time. So for Valentine's Day I had rented him a large garage that belonged to Cleveland's brother, Memphis, and Mac was finally building his boat.

"I wouldn't have asked you if I had romantic designs on Alfred tonight," Rose said with a saucy grin.

I glanced in the rearview mirror to see Mr. P.'s cheeks had turned pink. It was charming.

"All right, then yes," I said. "I would like to hear more about Gladstone House."

When he got home Elvis headed down the hall with Rose and Mr. P. I went into my apartment to drop my things and change. I washed my face and hands, brushed my hair and pulled on a pair of gray leggings and a loose sweater. I added a pair of fuzzy slipper boots, locked my door and padded down to Rose's apartment.

Mr. P. made a salad of lettuce, arugula, sprouts and carrots from the farmers market to go with our pasta. While we ate he told us what he'd learned about the history of Gladstone House.

"Emmeline Gladstone died more than a hundred

and seventy-five years ago," he said. "She was pledged to sea captain Joseph Phillips and she was waiting for him to return from a voyage so they could marry."

"Very romantic," I said.

"Rumors began swirling around North Harbor that Captain Phillips actually had a wife and family in another town and was just courting Emmeline for her money. The Gladstones were among the more affluent families in North Harbor at the time."

"Were the rumors true?" Rose asked.

"I haven't found the answer to that question yet," Mr. P. said. "It seems the same night that the captain returned to port, Emmeline was found dead."

I looked across the table at him. "Please don't tell me he killed her."

"At this point all I can tell you for certain was that Joseph Phillips was discovered kneeling by her body. He insisted that Emmeline had been dead when he arrived. The captain was arrested, tried and hanged for her murder, even as he insisted he was innocent to his last breath."

"So it's not really a romantic story at all," I said. "Emmeline was murdered and Captain Phillips either killed her or was hanged for a crime he didn't commit."

Mr. P. nodded. "People have been claiming they've seen Emmeline's ghost for decades. They believe they've seen her walking on the grounds or upstairs in a back bedroom looking out the window waiting for Captain Phillips."

"We see what we want to see," Rose said. "I do agree with Sarah, though. It's not a romantic story, more like a tragedy, but something about the idea of star-crossed lovers seems to appeal to people."

"You said some people think they've seen Emmeline's ghost looking out the window in a back bedroom," I said slowly.

Mr. P. gave me a knowing look. "I had the same thought. You said you spotted Mr. Steele's body in a back bedroom. From what you told me and what I know about the layout of the house from some photographs I saw, I think it was the same room."

"Coincidence?" I said.

Mr. P. raised an eyebrow. "When it comes to murder I'm not sure there are any coincidences."

Chapter 9

We finished eating and Rose talked a bit about the episodes of *Night Moves* that she had watched.

"As I said before, they have exposed quite a few charlatans," she said. Something about the tone of her voice told me she hadn't liked the show.

"But," I said, looking at her over the top of my water glass.

"But I found Mark Steele to be very aggressive in the more recent episodes of the show, almost as though he didn't just want to expose these people, he wanted to humiliate them as well. His co-host, Laurel Prescott, was nicer." She held up her fork before I could say anything. "I'm not saying I think that taking advantage of people is all right but I'm not a fan of public humiliation. I think we should have done away with that when we did away with public flogging."

"Have you talked to Laurel Prescott?"

Rose shook her head. "She's out of the country, but never fear, Alfred will track her down."

I wanted to help with the dishes, but Rose and Mr. P. presented a united front against that idea. United in the sense that not only did they refuse to let me help, they also stood side by side and kept me from reaching the sink. I knew I couldn't do an end run around both of them.

As soon as we were inside our apartment Elvis headed for the bedroom to watch *Jeopardy!* The cat had been a fan of the show as long as I'd had him. It was another one of his quirks like his inexplicable love for Elvis Presley's music—which was how he'd gotten his name—and his disdain for the Rolling Stones, which was why he wasn't called Mick.

After the death of Alex Trebek, Elvis had seemed confused by the parade of guest hosts. I hadn't told anyone because I felt foolish but I finally told the cat the *Jeopardy!* host was dead. Elvis had just stared at me with unblinking green eyes. For the next week he'd deliberately looked away from the television when *Jeopardy!* came on. The following Monday I'd turned on the TV wondering if the cat's *Jeopardy!* days were over, but this time Elvis had settled in to watch. As the weeks passed I'd gotten a kick out of his reaction to the different guest hosts. He'd showed a definite preference for LeVar Burton and Dr. Sanjay Gupta. Since Elvis had seen lots of *Next Generation* episodes with me, I understood his enthusiasm for the former. And now I wondered if he was secretly watching CNN, which might explain why he liked the latter.

While Elvis watched his show I went into the living room and called Liz. I explained that neither Mac nor I thought the furniture and appliances came from the camp.

For a moment Liz said nothing, then she sighed. "I thought the same thing. On paper it looks like Wilson wrote off everything and bought new. Channing is trying to figure out what he bought, when he bought it, who he bought it all from and most importantly where did the money come from."

I slid down on the sofa so I was sitting on my tailbone and thought how lucky I was to have Liam as a brother. He was trustworthy. He had integrity. He would never put me in the kind of mess that Wilson had left Liz in.

"Channing will figure it out," I said. "I think you should do nothing until you have those questions answered. You need to protect the foundation's good name and the camp."

"I'm glad my grandfather's not alive to see this," Liz said.

"If he were, he'd be proud of you for everything you're doing," I said. "And when you're ready we will do the cleanout if you still want us to."

"As Avery would say, you're my crew."

I laughed. "Back at you. Ride or die."

Now Liz was laughing. "We did a good job with you," she said.

I nodded even though she couldn't see me. "Yes, you did," I said.

Charlotte was working Thursday morning but Rose had decided to drive in with me to work on the case. When I stepped out into the hallway Mr. P. was waiting for us. "Good morning, Sarah," he said with a smile. "I trust it won't put you out if I ride with you."

I smiled back at him. "It won't. You're welcome any time."

"Thank you, my dear," he said. "I was going to walk but I'm not sure I could make it before the rain starts."

It was dull and cloudy outside. I had gone for a run right after I got up, and the air had that heavy feeling that suggested it was going to rain soon.

Rose came out of her apartment, smiling when she caught sight of us. "I'm sorry," she said. "I had to go back for sugar. I noticed we're getting low." She looked at me. "Sarah, did you get milk?"

I held up the canvas tote I was carrying. "Right here." The Angels ran on tea, generally with milk and sugar. I didn't want to think about what would happen if we ran out.

"First things first," I said once we were on the way to Second Chance. "We're not starting on Edgar's house tomorrow." Edgar was Mr. P.'s friend whose house we were supposed to clear out so he could put it on the market. Behind me I heard Mr. P. sigh softly.

"What happened?" Rose asked. She was in the front next to me and Elvis and Mr. P. were in the back.

"He met a woman."

"And what exactly is new in that?" she said.

"This one is serious."

Rose made a snort of disbelief. "And so were her twelve predecessors. Honestly I don't see what women see in him."

"Well, first of all, you always say there's a cover for

every pot," I said. Rose also added the caveat that if you couldn't find a cover for your pot you could always use a plate. That was where I kind of lost the point of the metaphor. "And number two, the man has all of his own teeth," I continued. "You're the one who seems to think that's important in a relationship." When Rose and the others had been trying to get Nick and me together the fact that I had all my own teeth and smelled good were two points in my favor.

"So you're using my own words against me?" she said.

I nodded. "I learned from the master." I flicked my gaze sideways to her. Her lips were pursed, not because she was annoyed but because she was clearly trying not to smile.

"So what's the plan for the day?"

"We need to talk to Annie and see if we can take a look around the house," Rose said.

"Annie has no reason to work with us," I said. I glanced in the rearview mirror. It seemed as though Mr. P. was showing the cat something on his phone.

"I disagree," Rose said. "It's to Annie's advantage to have the murder solved quickly and quietly. She's losing business right now. And it's not like she's a suspect. Even though she and Mr. Steele hadn't gotten along Annie couldn't have killed him. With her arthritis she hasn't been able to manage the stairs in that house in a long time."

"What about Emily?" I asked. "Not that I think she did it." I didn't really know Emily but she was a teaching assistant and she often helped with the hot lunch program at the elementary school. From what I'd seen she was thoughtful and kind. Not the sort of person who would stab someone with an ice pick.

"She didn't," Rose said.

I shot a quick glance her way. "And you know that because?"

"You said that Maud Fitch was at Gladstone House on Sunday."

"She was. She's one of the volunteers."

"I called her last night," Rose said. "Emily wasn't at the house when Mr. Steele was murdered. Annie had spilled tea all over the vintage lace tablecloth she'd put on the dining room table. She was upset. Annie can be very particular about things. Emily went to borrow a similar tablecloth from someone they knew. Her car broke down and she didn't get back to the house until after the police arrived. She was waiting for a tow truck when Mark Steele died."

"But we don't know when he died," I said.

"Well, we can certainly make an educated guess."

"We can?"

"Of course we can," she said. "It's simple math." She didn't say "try to keep up" but it was implied in her tone.

"Maud and Caroline Vega helped the Hastingses get the house ready in the morning. There wasn't much to do. The two of them headed out for lunch around twelve thirty and Emily left at the same time to get the tablecloth. Annie was tired and went to lie down for a while. At that point everything was in place. When they came back at quarter after one Maud says that

Emily had just called her grandmother about the car breaking down."

"I'm with you so far," I said.

"Maud told Annie they could set the table with another cloth," Rose said. "No one would notice. Maud retrieved the cloth from the back pantry, ironed it and set the table to Annie's instructions."

Elvis meowed again from the backseat.

"Good point," I said. "Elvis would like to know where Caroline was while Maud was setting the table."

"Elvis wants to know, does he?" she said.

I nodded. "He does."

"Emily had created a very lavish Victorian flower display with pink roses. It was in the parlor."

I frowned. "I don't remember seeing that."

"Because you didn't," Rose said. "The roses must have gotten cold because they were dead. While Maud was doing the table, Caroline went in search of candles and a candelabra to replace the flowers. She had to polish the candelabra. No one went upstairs but they were in and out of different rooms downstairs. There's isn't any way Mr. Steele could have gotten in the house then."

Mr. P. had been quiet up to now. "So you think Mr. Steele was already upstairs dead."

Goose bumps rose on my arms at the thought.

Rose shifted in her seat to look at Mr. P. "He had to have been killed earlier while Emily was gone, Maud and Caroline were at lunch and Annie was lying down. So that means he died in that forty-five-minute window between twelve thirty and quarter after one."

I couldn't see any flaw in her math but I could see one in her reasoning.

"How did he get in?" I asked.

"It was the middle of the day," Rose said. "I doubt the front door was locked. My best guess is that Mr. Steele showed up early to talk to Annie."

We were almost at the shop. "Okay," I said, "but then what? Did he happen upon some random person who stabbed him and then took off?"

"Maybe someone was with Mr. Steele and they argued," Mr. P. said.

"So this other person killed him in someone else's house where they could have been discovered at any moment? And—since I'm already playing devil's advocate—why didn't Annie hear them?"

"Annie and Emily live in a small apartment that's built on to the back of the house," Rose said. "She wouldn't have heard a thing back there. And as for why someone would have killed Mark Steele in someone else's house, maybe they didn't know they had killed him. Maybe they hadn't intended to kill him."

"Rosie makes a good point," Mr. P. said. "There was a case from about five years ago up in Bangor. Two young men had words outside a drinking establishment on a Thursday night. No punches were thrown but one pushed the other and walked off. The man who was pushed went backward and hit his head on the curb. He died two days later from a head injury. Maybe the person who killed Mr. Steele never intended to kill him and at least at the time didn't realize they had."

"I can't argue with your logic or Rose's," I said.

"Everything you've both said makes sense. But there's one problem with this whole scenario."

"And that is?" Mr. P. asked as we pulled into the lot.

I looked at him in the rearview mirror. "According to the way the two of you have laid things out, the most logical person to have killed Mark Steele would be our client. We only have Delia Watson's word that she was on the phone when Mark left. If the two of them had decided to try to ambush Annie or sneak into the house it's not like she's going to admit she was with him. Not if she's also responsible for his death."

"Yes, I know that, sweet girl," Rose said. "Before we do anything else we need to figure out whether or not our client is a killer."

Chapter 10

Charlotte was just arriving as I turned into the parking lot. She waited for us by the back door. Her cheeks were pink from her walk and I thought how happy she looked standing there in her bright tulip-red jacket and the cream-colored beanie that Rose had knit for her. Whoever Charlotte was seeing, it made me happy to see how *happy* the relationship was making her.

Mac came down the stairs without coffee for either one of us. "I'm sorry," he said. "I am running behind and the coffee isn't made."

"I'll take care of that," Mr. P. said, heading for the stairs. "And I'll put the kettle on for tea, Rosie," he said over his shoulder.

Rose and Charlotte were looking in the storage space under the stairs. Mac walked over to me and yawned. "I'm sorry," he said. "I swear it's not the company. I spent more time working on the boat than I meant to last night."

I loved the enthusiasm I could see in his eyes. I stretched up and kissed him. "Knowing you're working on your boat makes me happy."

He smiled. "Renting that garage from Memphis was the best gift I've ever gotten."

Rose and Charlotte headed upstairs and Mac and I went over what projects we needed to work on over the next few days.

"I'm going to work on those stools this morning," Mac said.

"Are you familiar with the phrase 'exercise in futility'?" I asked.

"O ye of little faith," he retorted, making a face at me.

"I have lots of faith in you," I said. "I also know that those stools are beyond fixing."

There was a sudden gleam in Mac's eye. "Care to make things a little interesting?"

"What did you have in mind?"

"A small wager." He gave an offhand shrug. "I work on the stools today and if I manage to get the dents out of at least two of them you will make me dinner. Place, time and menu to be decided by me."

I crossed my arms over my chest and met the challenge in his gaze with my own. The gauntlet had been thrown down. And I knew there was no way Mac was going to be able to permanently fix the dents in the seat of those stools. They were just too deep.

"And if you can't," I said, "then you make dinner for me. Same terms."

"Deal," he said, holding out his hand. He smiled. He was very confident and very deluded.

We shook hands.

Mr. P. came downstairs carrying a small tray with three cups of coffee. "Thank you," I said, taking one of them.

"Alfred, you are a lifesaver," Mac said. He gestured in the direction of the workshop with his coffee. "I'm going out to start working on those stools."

"Be careful," I said. "I don't want you to damage any fingers you may need when you're cooking."

"Would you mind if I tagged along?" Mr. P. asked. "I might have some ideas on how to solve your dented seat problem."

"You absolutely may tag along," Mac said. He smirked at me. "Two heads, Sarah."

"Need two hats," I retorted.

Rose and Charlotte came downstairs, each with a cup of tea because tea fueled everything they did.

"Charlotte has some information about the Gladstones," Rose said.

"I'd like to hear that," I said. I checked my watch. "There's time before we open."

"There's not a lot to tell," Charlotte said. "Annie Gladstone Hastings is an only child. The Gladstones had small families. She inherited the house from her father, Jacob Gladstone, who in turn inherited from his father, Henry Gladstone. They are all descended from Daniel Gladstone, who was Emmeline's only sibling."

"Who built the house?" I asked.

"Emmeline and Daniel's parents. Jacob added the small apartment at the back. Annie and Emily have been running the house as a bed-and-breakfast because its upkeep requires a lot of money and they can't afford to keep the house and pay the mortgage any other way."

Rose frowned. "Gladstone House is mortgaged?"

Charlotte nodded. "I was surprised to learn that, but I have it on good authority. It seems Annie had to mortgage the house years ago to pay for a new roof and repair other damage after a blizzard. She also spent some money on adding an extra bathroom and updating two others. She used to work as a nurse but lost her job when her arthritis meant she couldn't care for patients. I'm guessing she gets some kind of disability pension. From what I know of Annie she's probably been trying to juggle the finances all by herself for a long time."

"But she hasn't sold the house," I said. I took another sip of my coffee and made a mental note to ask Mr. P. about the coffee beans.

"Apparently she refuses to sell even though it would solve her financial problems. Maddie Hamilton was friends with Annie when they were in school. She told me that Annie sees the property as being Emily's legacy."

"I can understand that," Rose said. "Annie and Emily are the last of the Gladstone family," Rose said. She set her cup on the cash desk. "Maybe she believes that if Emily knows the house will be hers someday it might encourage her to have a family of her own, not to necessarily keep the Gladstone line going, but so Emily won't be without any family connections when Annie is gone."

"Family are the people you love who love you

back," I said quietly. "You don't have to have a biological connection."

Rose put a hand on my arm. "We know that," she said.

"Well, according to Maddie the only way Annie will be leaving that house is feetfirst," Charlotte said.

"Do you think business is good?" I asked. I set my coffee mug next to Rose's cup.

Charlotte shrugged. "They always seem to have a full house—even in the middle of winter. The food is excellent. Emily is an exceptional cook. And the idea that Emmeline is still waiting for Captain Phillips appeals to a lot of people even if it's not something the Hastingses actively promote."

"They had a lot to lose if Mark Steele managed to debunk the ghost story," I said.

A frown creased Charlotte's forehead. "But how would he have done that? Annie has never actively promoted the idea that Gladstone House is haunted by Emmeline's ghost so really what could he do?"

Rose seemed to be deep in thought, staring off into space. I waved a hand in front of her. "Rose, where did you go?" I said.

She shook her head. Then her eyes focused on my face. "What if Mark Steele had cast doubt on the love affair between Emmeline and Captain Phillips?" she said slowly. "What if he had been trying to expose the whole story as a fabrication? It works now because most people believe the captain was unjustly convicted and put to death. They don't believe he had another family and they certainly don't believe he killed Emmeline."

"So you think Captain Phillips *did* murder Emmeline?" Charlotte said.

"It's possible he was in fact a scoundrel and a reprobate. What if the show didn't just want to debunk the ghost story? What if they wanted to debunk the idea of the captain as a tragic figure? What if the whole 'love story' was nothing but a fairy tale?"

"In that case Annie and Emily are the two most likely suspects," I said, "and we know both of them have alibis."

Rose tipped her head to one side. When she did that she reminded me of a tiny, inquisitive bird. "What about the Phillips family?"

Charlotte glanced at her watch. "So some descendant of Captain Phillips killed Mr. Steele? Would they actually care that much after so much time has passed?"

"Yes," I said, thinking of how much Liz didn't want the Emmerson Foundation name tarnished because it would affect the legacy of her beloved grandfather. "And maybe Mark Steele wasn't deliberately murdered. His death may well have been an accident, something that happened because of an argument. I think we need to know more about Captain Phillips's family."

"You should talk to your grandmother," Charlotte said. "She worked on planning the house tour for months. She may know more about the history of Gladstone House."

I nodded. "I will."

"Will you talk to Clayton?" Rose asked Charlotte. Clayton McNamara was my friend Glenn's uncle. He was also a walking encyclopedia when it came to the history of North Harbor.

"Of course," Charlotte said. She looked at me. "I'll go open up."

"I'm going to do some digging online to see who had a beef with Mark Steele," Rose said.

I nodded. "And I'm going to check for new website orders."

I spent about half an hour working in my office. When I went back downstairs, Charlotte was sweeping the floor and looking very pleased with herself.

"Do you notice anything?" she asked.

I looked around. "The rocking chair is gone."

"Yes it is," she said, beaming at me.

I put my hands on my hips. "Charlotte Elliot, you've been holding out on me. You obviously have a magic wand in your apron pocket."

She laughed.

"Seriously," I said. "What did you do?"

"Well, I tried a bunch of pillow, teddy bear and blanket permutations but none of them worked. Right after you went upstairs a man and woman came in— brother and sister. He was looking for a set of wine-glasses to replace a set that got broken in a move as a gift for his husband. The story seemed to involve poor packing, an insubstantial box, an untrained dog and a perceived lack of sentimentality."

"In other words your guy didn't pack the glasses well, their dog which is more his dog knocked the box over, glasses were important to husband who is very sentimental—your guy is not. He's been looking for replacement glasses to show how sorry he is probably as a gift for their anniversary." I held out both hands, palms up. "How am I doing so far?"

"You're dead-on," she said. "How did you know?"

"It's not the first time I've heard some version of that story," I said. "Did you find the wineglasses?"

"In the third box we checked. Meanwhile his sister spent the entire time in the chair. When she got up she said she was buying it. She made her brother carry it out to his SUV. She carried the glasses because, as she explained it, the dog isn't the only one in the family that's clumsy." She waved the broom. "Abracadabra and the rocker is gone."

I poked my head in the Angels' office before I headed out to the garage workshop to see how the un-denting was going. Elvis was sitting on Mr. P.'s desk and the cat and Rose were looking at the computer screen.

"Knock, knock," I said.

"Perfect timing," she said. "Are you available after lunch?"

"I am," I said. "What do you need?"

"I need to go over to the Strathmore Inn. It's where Mark Steele and Delia Watson were staying. I want to find out if she was where she said she was Sunday afternoon."

"Has she checked out?" It didn't seem like it would be a good thing to run into our client while we were looking into her alibi.

"She hasn't," Rose said. "But she'll be gone all afternoon. I looked at her social media. She's going to visit a so-called haunted house down the coast somewhere."

"What time do you want to leave?" I asked. Elvis was still studying the computer screen.

"One thirty, if that works for you."

"It does," I said.

Rose smiled. "Thank you, sweetie."

I headed outside. Mac and Mr. P. were in front of the old garage wearing goggles and heavy work gloves. Mac appeared to be heating the top of one of the stools with a hair dryer. He looked at Mr. P. who nodded in return. Mac turned off the hair dryer and stepped back. Mr. P. was holding some device that looked like a cross between a toilet plunger and pressure washer. It was connected to an air compressor. He pressed the plunger-like end down on the top of the stool. Mac flicked on the air compressor and after a moment there was a loud bang that almost knocked the old man off his feet. Mr. P.'s machine, whatever it was, seemed to have worked. The dent in the top of the stool was gone. They high-fived each other and grinned.

"What is that thing?" I asked as I joined them.

"The Dento 5000," Mr. P. said, holding up his contraption with a fair amount of pride.

Up close it looked like something I'd seen in an episode of the original *Star Trek*. "Where did you get it?"

The men exchanged a look. "It's the result of a foray into late-night infomercial shopping," Mr. P. said.

They looked like a pair of little boys standing there: a little bit guilty and a whole lot proud. All they needed was a bit of dirt on their faces and some grass stains on their pants.

"Just don't hurt yourselves," I said.

"We're not going to hurt ourselves," Mac said. "This thing is amazing. This is the second stool we've fixed. I think we need our own."

At that exact moment there was a loud bang as one of the stools re-dented. Mac and Mr. P. looked at each other.

I didn't say a word. I did take two steps back, however.

"We can fix that," Mac said. And then the second stool gave a loud bang and rolled about a foot in my direction.

Mr. P. shook his head. "Alas, it seems late-night TV and a credit card don't always result in good decisions. The blanket with sleeves might have been the better choice."

I looked at Mac. He looked a little sheepish. "Lasagna," I said. "And brownies. No nuts." I turned and headed for the shop.

"The day's not over yet," Mac called after me.

"Lasagna," I repeated, without looking back.

Chapter 11

Rose and I drove over to the Strathmore Inn after lunch. It was a beautiful old building—one of my favorites in North Harbor. Over the years it had been meticulously restored and furnished and I was always hoping that it would turn up on the spring house tour some year just so I could get a close look at the furniture and other details in the various rooms.

I didn't recognize the young man working at the reception desk. More importantly, neither did Rose. And that turned out to be a problem. Because he also seemed to be immune to her charm. He very politely refused to tell us anything about Mark Steele or Delia Watson even after Rose had explained why we were there and given him her business card.

"The privacy of our visitors is paramount," he said. There was a faint touch of a British accent in his voice. Even though I hadn't worked in radio in years I still noticed people's voices.

"You know he's going to tell Delia that there were

people here asking about her," I said as we walked back to the car.

Rose nodded. "That's why I said we were looking for information on her and Mr. Steele."

I was just unlocking Rose's door when someone called, "Mrs. Jackson!"

We both turned in the direction the voice had come from. A young woman was hurrying toward us from the other end of the parking area.

"Mrs. Jackson, I knew that was you," she said as she got closer to us.

Rose smiled and caught the young woman's hands in hers. "Rosalie," she exclaimed. "What a wonderful surprise. What are you doing here?"

"I work here part-time as a maid," she said, "and I'm a year away from finishing my degree. Premed."

"I'm so proud of you," Rose said. "You'll be a wonderful doctor." She turned to me. "Sarah, this is Rosalie Leclair. She was one of my students."

I smiled. "It's nice to meet you." Rosalie was petite and curvy with dark hair in a thick braid and dark eyes. I realized I'd seen her in the library several times and at the Thursday Night Jam at The Black Bear pub.

"You too," she said. "Mrs. Jackson was my favorite teacher."

"I've heard that before," I said.

"Mrs. Jackson, is it true that you're a private detective now?" Rosalie asked.

Rose nodded. "Yes, I am."

Rosalie looked at me. "I know Mrs. Jackson must be good at it because no one could ever hide things from her when she was a teacher."

"I've known her all my life and I've never been able to fool her on anything," I said.

Rose patted my arm. "Don't give me all the credit," she said. "You are a terrible liar."

"Are you investigating Mr. Steele's death?" Rosalie asked.

Rose glanced at me. "We are," she said. "Did you meet him?"

She nodded. "I cleaned his room . . . let me see . . . three times. He was my favorite kind of guest. He never left a mess and when he wanted an extra towel, he asked instead of just taking one from my cart, *and* he said please and thank you. He did seem kind of intense, though."

"Intense how?" I asked.

Rosalie shrugged. "He was always on his phone having some sort of serious conversation. He'd be frowning and gesturing with one hand. I met him once in the hallway and I saw him out here a couple of times."

"Did you see Mr. Steele with his producer?" Rose asked.

"The woman? Yes, a couple of times. She was always on her phone, too—or her computer. And her room was a disaster area. She left wet towels on the floor and the bed. Her clothes were everywhere and she had these fur-trimmed gloves that she left in the bathroom. The first time I saw one I thought it was a rat and I beat on it with my vacuum." She shook her head. "She was in her room a lot over the weekend. One time I had to work around her but she didn't seem to mind and she was a good tipper."

"Was that Saturday or Sunday?" Rose asked.

"Sunday. I worked all day Saturday, but I didn't see Mr. Steele or his producer. On Sunday I saw him leave about twelve thirty. He was talking to a man right out here and then he got into his car."

"Rosalie, do you remember what the man Mr. Steele was talking to looked like?" Rose asked.

The young woman thought for a moment, a frown creasing her forehead. "I didn't really get a good look at him. I was at the back door shaking a couple of mats. One of the light poles pretty much blocked my view. He was just average, shorter than Mr. Steele."

"And no one left with Mr. Steele? Not his producer? Not anyone else?"

"No. Like I said, I had to clean the room with her in it and I went to do that right after I shook those mats. It was my last room and I wanted to get finished." She smiled. "Does any of this help?"

"It does," Rose said. "Thank you. I'm so happy you're doing well."

"Thank you for always believing in me," Rosalie said, wrapping Rose in a hug.

We said good-bye and climbed into the car. "It looks like our client isn't guilty after all," I said.

"Are you sorry?" Rose asked as she fastened her seat belt.

"Well, it would have made solving the case pretty darned easy."

"The easy answer is seldom the right one," she said. "What I'd like to know is who the man was that Rosalie saw with Mr. Steele."

"That sounds like Mr. P.'s department," I said as I backed out of our parking spot.

"I'll get him working on it when we get back." She paused.

"I can hear all the little gears turning in your head," I said. "What are you thinking?"

"Are we in a hurry?"

I shook my head. "I'm not."

"What if we stopped at Gladstone House? We need to talk to Annie and there's no time like the present."

"Let's do it," I said.

I parked on the street in the same place Michelle had parked when we'd been there on Sunday. We climbed the front steps and Rose rang the bell. We waited and then Annie Hastings opened the door. "Rose Jackson," she said. "What took you so long?"

Annie led us into the dining room. She moved slowly but steadily, leaning on her cane. "I just put the kettle on," she said. "Will you join me in a cup of tea?"

"If it's not too much trouble," Rose said.

Annie made a dismissive gesture with one hand. "It's not."

"May I help you carry things?" I asked.

"Yes, you may," she said. "Thank you." She looked at Rose. "Have a seat. We'll be right back."

I followed Annie back to the kitchen. She plugged in the electric kettle to bring the water back to a boil. The kitchen had clearly been modernized but lots of historical details had been left. I was guessing that most if not all of the trim was new, but it had been milled to match the existing woodwork. Along one wall was a huge walnut hutch that someone had spent a lot of hours sanding and refinishing.

Annie followed my gaze. "It's original to the house."

"It's a beautiful piece of furniture."

"Isabel said you have an old house yourself." She took a large tray from a nearby cupboard.

"I do," I said. "But mine is divided into three apartments."

"Your grandmother and her husband live in one of them."

I nodded. "Yes, they do. And Rose lives in the other."

Annie laughed. "How does that work for you?"

"Honestly, better than I expected," I said.

Annie made the tea in a beautiful china teapot covered in tiny blue forget-me-nots and then covered the pot with a quilted blue and gray cozy. She put a matching pitcher of milk and a sugar bowl on the tray along with spoons, three cups with saucers and a plate of cookies. I carried everything back to the dining room.

Rose was looking at a framed black-and-white photo hanging on the far end wall. I wondered how much looking around she'd done while we'd been in the kitchen. "How old is this photo?" she asked.

"More than a hundred years," Annie said. "My best guess on the date is somewhere just either side of 1895."

I walked over to join Rose. The photograph was of several men standing on what looked to be a makeshift bridge over a river. They were all holding some sort of pitchfork.

"What are they doing?" I said.

"They're cutting ice," Annie replied. She took the cozy off the pot and began to pour the tea.

Rose and I took seats at the long table. "I remember my father talking about cutting ice on the Kennebec River one winter. He was about eighteen."

"Mine as well," Annie said. "Now we think it's a hardship if our refrigerators don't have an ice maker."

The cookies were butterscotch oatmeal and she offered them to Rose and me. I thanked her, took one and broke it into two pieces taking a bite from one of them.

"These are delicious," I said. The cookies were thin and crispy with just the right amount of butterscotch goodness.

"Emily made them. I'll tell her you liked them." She took a sip of her tea, then folded her hands in her lap and looked across the table at Rose. "Fire away," she said.

"Why were you against Mark Steele featuring Gladstone House on his television show?" Rose said.

"Have you seen the show?" Annie asked.

"Yes."

"Then you know what Mr. Steele was like. He wasn't happy until he had humiliated everyone." She paused. "Do either of you believe in ghosts?"

I shook my head. Rose said no.

"Neither do I," Annie said, reaching for her cup again. "But believing makes some people happy, in some cases gives them comfort and who does it hurt? I don't support people charging money for fake Ouija board messages or séances with messages that come from the dead, but if someone stays at Gladstone House and thinks they see Emmeline and that restores their faith in true love is that so bad?"

"Mr. Steele didn't take no for an answer," Rose said.

Annie took a sip of her tea and nodded. "I said no to him the first time he contacted me. And the second time and every subsequent attempt. When he wouldn't give up I blocked his calls and his emails. Emily did the same. He tried to get around me by having his producer call but we're not as clueless as the big-city folk seem to think we are."

"Did you see Mr. Steele or hear from him on Sunday?" Rose asked.

Annie shook her head. "I did not. I had no idea he was in town and no idea that he'd bought tickets under a fake name."

"Do you have any idea what he was doing here?" I asked.

"The same thing he's been doing for months," she said with a dismissive wave of her hand. "Trying to wear me down. I didn't kill the man because I couldn't have gotten up the stairs to do it. But I can't promise I wouldn't have whacked him with my cane if I'd seen him. And for the record, Emily couldn't have killed Mr. Steele because she wasn't even here."

She reached for the teapot and added a little to her cup and to Rose's. She gave me an inquiring look and I shook my head.

"What Mark Steele was doing was harassment, pure and simple. I talked to a lawyer and had him draft a letter to the show. Given what happened to Mr. Steele

I've held off on sending it but I still plan to. Talk to my lawyer. You probably know him. Joshua Evans."

"We know him," Rose said.

We knew Josh quite well. He had gotten the Angels out of more than one scrape and represented more than one of their clients. And his mother, Jane, was Liz's executive assistant.

"Do you know if there are any living descendants of Captain Phillips?" I asked.

"If you're asking if the stories that he already had a wife and family somewhere were true, they weren't," Annie said.

"I wasn't," I said. "I just wondered whether Mr. Steele had tried to approach the captain's family since he seemed so determined to tell this story."

Her expression softened. "Joseph had no children so there are no direct descendants, but he did have a younger sister. The family left North Harbor not long after Joseph was hanged and I have no idea what happened to them." She turned her cup in its saucer. "I suspect everyone connected to him is long dead because Mark Steele was so fixated on Emmeline's story I think he would have dug up a distant relative if there was one to find." She glanced at the fireplace mantel. "Would you like to see a picture of Emmeline?"

"Yes," Rose and I both answered.

Annie got to her feet and made her way over to the fireplace. She took a small picture frame from the mantel and came back to the table, offering it to me. Rose leaned in to get a closer look.

Emmeline Gladstone had been a beautiful young

woman. In the photo there was a slight smile on her face. Her hair was pulled back in a bun. She had fair skin and light-colored eyes—probably blue or green. She was wearing what looked to be a full skirt with a fitted jacket with possibly velvet cuffs and a stand-up collar. She looked happy.

I looked up at Annie. "She's smiling. In every photo I've seen from that time frame everyone looks so stern."

A smile played across Annie's face. "Family lore has it that Emmeline was always smiling and it was impossible to get an image of her when she wasn't."

There wasn't much more to say. We thanked Annie for the tea and her time. I offered to carry everything back to the kitchen but she waved my help away. "Emily will take care of that when she gets home."

"Thank you for talking to us," Rose said.

"I can't say I'm that sorry the man is dead," Annie said. "But I hope you find the killer soon. It will make my life easier."

We headed back to Second Chance. Rose seemed to be deep in thought.

"What's on your mind?" I asked after a couple of minutes of silence.

"Most of the time someone thinks they've seen a ghost, they haven't," she said.

"All of the time because there's no such thing as ghosts."

Rose nodded. "Exactly. A lot of the time it's just wishful thinking coupled with a trick of the light, a drafty window making a curtain flutter, old wiring that causes a light to flicker."

"Yes."

"But, Sarah, sometimes a light bulb is loosened to make it flicker. A stair tread is tampered with to make it suddenly creak when it didn't before. A gossamer scarf on a tree branch creates the illusion that someone is standing in the darkness."

"What are you saying?" I asked.

"I think the Hastingses have been staging the encounters with Emmeline's ghost."

I shot a quick glance in her direction. As usual Rose was sitting calmly in the seat, hands folded in her lap.

"Why on earth do you think that?"

"As I told you Mark Steele was obsessive and aggressive but if Annie had nothing to hide what did it matter what he did? I understand that it must have been annoying to have Mr. Steele refuse to take no for an answer but maybe the reason Annie wanted nothing to do with the show was because he was right. Maybe there was something to find."

Chapter 12

When Rose and I got back to Second Chance we discovered that Mac and Mr. P. were still working on the metal stools. They had one wedged on its side and Mac was trying to pound out the dents in the stool from the underside. It didn't look like it was working.

"They are persistent," Rose said as we made our way to the back door. "Misguided but persistent."

While we were gone Avery had finished packing the picnic baskets. She had already washed them with the hose and set them to dry overnight. She and Rose had decided to put a small blanket in each basket instead of a tablecloth.

"I thought it would be a good use for those gray and white cotton blankets," Rose said. The blankets had been part of the contents of a storage space I'd bought a while ago. They were soft and warm but they hadn't sold, maybe because they were small—just twin size.

The baskets were packed with real cutlery, two

wineglasses, china plates, cloth napkins, a bottle opener, the menu from Glenn's bakery—Avery laminated each one at the copy shop—a coupon for a discount from the sandwich shop bakery, which was Glenn's idea, and a bottle of sparkling, nonalcoholic wine. Avery had done an excellent job on the presentation, tying the cutlery and napkins together with wide ribbon, fastening tiny paper flowers she'd made from the pages of an old book to the wine bottle.

"You did an excellent job," I told her. "These baskets are even better than I'd hoped. And I like the extra little touches like the bottle opener."

"I didn't really do that much," Avery said with a shrug. "It was Rose's idea."

Rose beamed at her. "It may have been my idea but you took it and ran with it. I'm proud of you." She wrapped Avery in a hug. The teen looked a little embarrassed but I noticed she didn't pull away.

We stepped into the store proper. "Perfect timing," Charlotte said. She was with a customer who looked to be in his midtwenties. He was checking out our selection of guitars. "Tell me about this one," he said, pointing to my latest find.

I lifted the instrument down from the wall and offered it to him. Once someone played one of our guitars they were more likely to buy it.

"This is a Seagull guitar," I told him. "They're made in Canada. The top is solid spruce and the sides and back are cherry."

He tried a couple of chords, adjusted the tuning a little and then played something I quickly recognized as Neil Young's "Long May You Run." I saw a smile play across the man's face and I knew I'd made a sale.

A couple of weekends ago Mac and I had driven down to Port Clyde to see a man who was building his third wooden boat. While they talked I had spent some time prowling around a flea market that was being held at the local high school. I'd spotted the guitar in a back corner of one of the booths. I'd offered forty dollars for it, seeing the amount as a point to start dickering over the price. To my surprise my offer was accepted. The woman running the booth wrapped the guitar in a large blue recycling bag and as she took my money something about her smile and the gleam in her eye gave me the feeling that as far as she was concerned she was the one who had gotten the deal.

The rest of the afternoon was busy. Right after the guitar player left, a tour bus returning home to Nova Scotia after a couple of days in Atlantic City stopped in. Two of the picnic baskets sold, along with several of the framed maps, a set of dishes that Rose and Avery carefully packed for the bus ride home, and a small table I swaddled in an old moving blanket, which Mr. P. and the bus driver managed to fit in the luggage compartment of the bus in a space that it really shouldn't have fit in but somehow did.

Rose updated everyone on what we had learned about Delia and her suspicions about the Hastingses and the ghost sightings of Emmeline. Charlotte seemed a little skeptical. "What you're really saying is that it's Emily behind the hauntings and if that's the case it means she's a much better liar than I would have believed."

After the tour bus left I went up to my office and tried my grandmother. Since it was Thursday I'd be down at The Black Bear for the jam and I wanted to hear what she knew about the Gladstones and the Phillipses sooner rather than later.

"Hi, sweetie. How are you?" Gram said when she answered.

"I'm fine. I'm calling to pick your brain," I said.

"You're welcome to whatever you can find in there," she said. I pictured her smiling on the other end of the phone.

"What do you know about Annie Hastings and the Gladstone family?"

"Not that much. My father always said they were house poor. Annie's father worked as the postmaster. It was a steady job but they had that house to keep up. You've been inside. You know how big it is."

"What about her mother?" The door to my office swung open and a moment later Elvis launched himself onto my desk. He padded over to sit in front of me. I reached up to stroke his fur and he started to purr.

"Annie's mother did not come into the marriage with any dowry," Gram said. "She was a talented seamstress and worked on party gowns and wedding dresses for extra money but, so the story goes, she was so meticulous about her work that she didn't make very much."

"Annie was an only child, wasn't she?" I said.

"She was the only child her parents had that survived. They had a baby girl before Annie that was stillborn and little boy born when she was about two who died when he was less than a month old."

I had a sudden lump in my throat. "That's so sad and so unfair."

Gram sighed. "Sometimes life works that way. I remember my mother saying that the family kept very much to themselves, especially after their baby boy died. I think it must have been difficult to live in that house, surrounded by the homes of all those wealthy people and, because of a ridiculous class system, always be an outsider."

Elvis jumped down onto my lap. He nudged my hand with his head and I took the hint and gave him a scratch behind his right ear.

"Do you know anything about the Phillips family?" I said.

"I'm sorry, sweetie, I don't," Gram said. "The story was always that the family left North Harbor under a cloud of shame. It's probably worth talking to Clayton. He is the keeper, so to speak, of all the old stories about North Harbor."

"Rose is a step ahead of you. She's already asked Charlotte to see what Clayton knows."

"If he doesn't know anything I don't know who else you could talk to. Someone should save all those stories for future generations while Clayton is still around."

"How did Clayton end up knowing so much of the town's history?" I asked.

"Oh, that was because of his grandmother, Evelyn," Gram said. "Not to speak ill of the dead but that woman was a gossip. Evelyn knew everything about everyone. Clayton spent a lot of time with her. I think he just acquired all he knows kind of by osmosis though he does have a lot of her papers."

I talked to Gram for a couple more minutes, telling her all about Mac and Mr. P.'s efforts to fix the stools. I said good-bye with a promise that I'd come to dinner soon.

I passed on what I had learned to Mr. P. He was already trying to find out who the man was that Rosalie had seen with Mark Steele.

"I've been looking up the neighbors in the vicinity of the Strathmore in the hopes of finding some security camera footage," he said. He smiled and nudged his glasses up his nose. "All aboveboard of course."

"Great," I said, hoping his search stayed that way.

I went out to the workshop to see how Mac was doing with the stools. They actually looked worse than they had before he'd started his efforts to undent the seats.

"Okay, so I may have been a little overzealous with the mallet," Mac said, a bit of a hangdog expression on his face.

There was no one around so I kissed him. "Lasagna and brownies," I said, patting his cheek. "I know Rose will bail you out and make the brownies but because I am such a gracious winner I'm going to let that slide."

Mac laughed. "Saturday night?" he asked.

I nodded.

"My place or yours?"

"Mine," I said. "Bring your toothbrush."

Mac was going to work on the boat for a couple of hours. Cleveland was joining him. Liz came to pick up Avery along with Rose and Mr. P. They were all going out to dinner. They were discussing where to go as I locked the front door and scooped up Elvis.

"I am not eating kale and bean curd," Liz said in response to Avery's suggestion that they try the new vegetarian restaurant that had opened.

"There's nothing wrong with trying new things," Rose said. "You need to have a more open mind."

"They have coconut bacon, Nonna," Avery said.

"I like my bacon from pigs, thank you very much," Liz said. "And I'll have you all know that I do have an open mind but not so open my brains come out my nose."

Avery grinned over her shoulder at me and I realized she was enjoying the debate.

"Could I give you a ride?" I asked Charlotte.

"Yes, please," she said. The wind had come up and it looked a lot colder outside.

"Do you think Rose is right about Annie and Emily somehow faking the sightings of Emmeline?" I asked as we pulled out of the parking lot.

"I'm not sure." Out of the corner of my eye I could see she was frowning. "But even if they were, that doesn't mean it has anything to do with Mark Steele's murder other than it put Gladstone House in his sights."

"I think we need to move beyond the obvious."

Elvis loudly meowed his agreement.

"What are the two of you thinking?" Charlotte said.

"Given the type of show *Night Moves* is and the kind of person Mark Steele seems to have been, maybe we should take a closer look at some of the people he exposed. To steal one of Rose's expressions, maybe someone had an axe to grind."

I dropped off Charlotte and Elvis and I headed for home. The cat settled in to watch *Jeopardy!* I took a quick shower and changed into jeans, a long-sleeved T-shirt and a V-neck pullover. I decided to have supper at the pub.

I drove down and managed to find a parking spot close to The Black Bear. When I stepped inside the pub I spotted Sam across the room talking to the bartender. I walked over to say hello. I caught sight of Jess at our favorite table talking to Josh. I waved and pointed at Sam so she knew what I was doing. She nodded and went back to her conversation.

Sam's dollar-store glasses were perched on the end of his nose. His shaggy hair, a mix of gray and blond, was past due for a haircut.

He smiled. "Hey, kiddo," he said.

"Hey, yourself," I said, giving him a hug. I thought about how lucky I was compared to Annie and Emily. I had a big family of people who loved me and who I loved back just as much. And they were my family even though most of them weren't related to me or to one another.

Sam had been my father's best friend and even though Peter Kennelly had been my dad for most of my life Sam filled a role that no one else did or could because he had known my biological dad so well.

Whenever I missed my father, which didn't happen as much now as it had when I was a kid, it was Sam I sought out.

"I hear the Angels have a case," Sam said. "Stay safe, okay?"

I nodded. "I promise."

He smiled again. "How about some morning you come down and I'll make you breakfast. You can bring Elvis."

"I will," I said. I looked around. "It's almost time for you to give your fans what they came for."

"You mean a bunch of old guys singing old rock and roll?"

"Hey, 'it's gotta be rock and roll music if you wanna dance with me,'" I said. I gave him another hug and whispered, "Love you."

"You too, kiddo," he said.

I made my way over to Josh and Jess. I'd known Josh since we were kids and the grown-up Josh was a lot like Josh the kid. He was smart and persistent and deeply loyal. He could have practiced law anywhere, but North Harbor was home and in the end it had pulled him back much the way it had me.

"Annie Hastings called me," he said without pre-amble. "She gave me permission to tell you that she did come to see me last week about sending a letter to Mark Steele and the producers of *Night Moves* telling them to leave the Hastingses alone and to stay away from Gladstone House."

"That was a pretty severe step," I said.

"They didn't seem to understand the meaning of

no. Mr. Steele in particular. To him it seemed to mean push harder." He smiled. "If you have any other questions you know where to find me."

"I do," I said. "Thanks."

"Take care," he said to Jess and then he went to join his friends.

"Hi," Jess said.

"Hi back at you," I said.

She gave me a hug before sitting back down. "Any luck with the new case?"

I shook my head. "Not yet." I pulled off my jacket and hung it on the back of my chair before I sat down. "But you know Rose. She doesn't give up easily."

"She doesn't give up period," Jess said.

"Before I forget I'll take more pillows as soon as you have any."

Her long, dark hair was in a thick braid and she flipped it over her shoulder. "It may be a while. I'm working on two wedding dresses—both remakes. One belonged to the bride's grandmother—the hand beading is incredible—and the other was a thrift store find that seems to be very good quality. The tags are gone so I have no idea where it came from or how old it is."

Jess was a very talented seamstress. Word was getting around about her skill at making wedding dresses, whether it was reworking a vintage gown or coming up with a totally new design. It struck me I should just ask her what happened on Valentine's Day with Nick. Jess and I had been friends for a long time, too long to have this . . . secret hanging between us. I started to say something when Nick dropped into the chair beside me.

"Miss me?" he asked.

"You're in a good mood," I said. His hair was damp at the ends like he'd just gotten out of the shower a short while ago, which he probably had.

"I'm always in a good mood."

Jess gave a snort of laughter and I rolled my eyes.

"Would you get us a waiter?" I said to Jess. "I'm hungry."

She leaned behind me, raised an eyebrow and out of nowhere a waiter started toward us. I had no idea how she did that. It was just her superpower.

I ordered a chicken burger and fries. "Have you eaten?" I asked Nick.

He frowned. "I had lunch . . . I think."

"Make that two chicken burgers with fries," I told the waiter. I also ordered a large platter of salsa and chips. It was kind of our tradition.

"Thank you," Jess said with a smile.

Nick leaned back in his chair. He was wearing jeans and a black hoodie. "Have you caught the bad guy yet?" he asked.

"Hey, don't be sexist," Jess said. "Women can kill, too."

He held up one hand. "I stand corrected. Have you caught the bad guy or girl yet?"

"You mean you didn't read Rose's update?" I teased.

He shook his head. "You're joking but she does text me with updates on the case."

I shrugged one shoulder. "You're part of the team."

"I don't want to be part of the team," he said. "I already have a team . . . sort of." He raked a hand back through his hair. "You know what I mean."

Jess and I both laughed. "It's like being in the mob," she said. "Once you're part of the Angels' team you're part of it forever."

"Have either of you ever seen *Night Moves*?" I asked.

"Yeah," Jess said.

Nick nodded.

"So did you like it?"

"For the first couple of episodes, but then I noticed how Mark Steele seemed to enjoy exposing people and embarrassing them," Jess said. "And I didn't like the way he treated the people who were scammed, who believed in ghosts. He acted as though they were stupid for thinking it could be real."

"I thought the same thing," Nick said. "Although I don't believe in ghosts. If they're real why don't they just appear and say here I am?"

Jess was nodding. "Exactly. They're always haunting old spooky houses after dark. They never appear in the middle of the day when the sun is shining."

"I'm with Jess," Nick said. "I didn't like the way he seemed to be making fun of the people who do believe. He seemed to be implying it was their fault they got conned."

"So maybe one of those people killed him," Jess said. She leaned an elbow on the table and propped her head on her hand.

"Mark Steele died from a pneumothorax, right?" I said to Nick. "So that basically means his lung collapsed."

He nodded. "There was a puncture wound in his chest. Air leaked into the space between his chest wall and his lung." He put one hand on the left side of his chest. "That air pushed on the outside of his lung."

"And that's what made it collapse."

"Yes." It was the same explanation Delia Watson had given us.

"It doesn't sound like a very nice way to die," Jess said.

Nick blew out a breath. "It's not."

"If you were killing someone, how would you do it?" I asked.

"I *wouldn't* kill anyone," he said.

I jabbed his side with my elbow. "I know that. I'm talking theoretically or hypothetically, whichever word works best for you."

He thought for a moment. "I'd make it look like an accident. If I was going to kill someone I wouldn't want to go to prison."

"So you probably wouldn't stab your victim with an ice pick."

"Kind of hard to say that happened accidentally." He narrowed his gaze. "You think Mark Steele's murder was spur-of-the-moment."

"And you don't?"

"I didn't say that," Nick said. "Maybe his death was planned days in advance. Or maybe minutes ahead. Maybe his killer struck in anger or out of fear. It doesn't matter. If you want to figure out who killed Mark Steele figure out who benefits. Whether it's in the moment of the murder or it's after, find the answer to that question. Who benefits?"

Chapter 13

Sam ended the night's music with his version of Bob Seger's "We've Got Tonight." By that point pretty much everyone in the pub was on their feet. Jess was leaning her head against mine while my head was against Nick's shoulder and all three of us were swaying to the music. I could hear Nick singing along very softly in my ear and I wished I could convince him to get up and perform with Sam and the boys. Anyone was welcome to join them. Nick had done that in the past but it had been a while. He was a good guitar player and he had a decent voice as well, but when I brought up joining Sam for a song he'd just laugh off the suggestion.

"I'll see you at Mom's on Sunday for dinner, right?" Nick said as he pulled on his jacket.

"Of course," I said. Charlotte tried to get us all together for dinner fairly regularly and since she was a great cook—and great company—I never said no.

"Me too," Jess said, waving the end of the red and black scarf she was winding around her neck.

I made a circle that included all three of us with one finger. "Dish duty?"

"Absolutely," Jess said.

Nick nodded.

I dropped Jess off and headed home. Elvis was still in residence in the chair in the bedroom except now he was sprawled on his back with his head hanging partway off the seat. He yawned but made no effort to move.

"I might want to sit there and watch the late news," I said. He yawned again and closed his green eyes. I was being ignored.

The next morning Elvis was my only companion on the drive to the shop. He was also a more picky backseat driver than usual. He found something wrong with the way I stopped at the stop sign at the corner. I didn't seem to put on my turn signal when he thought I should and once he leaned sideways almost as though he was looking at the speedometer.

I remembered the first time I'd seen Elvis. It had been down at the pub because Sam had been feeding him. Elvis had just turned up down along the harbor front one day. Sam wasn't sure if he'd been with someone who had been passing through and Elvis had run off or if the cat had been abandoned. No one had ever come looking for him.

The vet who checked out Elvis after Sam more or less tricked me into taking the cat said he was in good health but he had at some point been hurt in a fight. There was the scar across his nose that gave him a bit of bad boy charm but there were others under his fur that had come from deeper, longer wounds. He was very friendly and charmed pretty much everyone who came into Second Chance. Elvis had even won over more than one person who wasn't a cat fan. And he and Rose, working together, could sell just about anything. I hadn't wanted a cat and I hadn't even been sure I could take care of one. But I was happy that I had him in my life.

As usual Elvis wanted to be carried across the parking lot. "I'm not carrying you," I said. We did a brief stare-down. He put one paw on my messenger bag, lying on the seat next to him. He didn't blink even once. "Oh, for heaven's sake," I muttered, scooping up the cat with one hand and my bag with the other. He gave a little self-satisfied sigh and licked the side of my face.

Liz pulled into the parking lot then. Charlotte was with her.

Charlotte smiled as she climbed out of the passenger side of the car. "Good morning," she said.

Elvis meowed an enthusiastic hello.

I smiled back at her. "Good morning."

"Liz wants a word with you," Charlotte said. She looked at Elvis. "Let's go," she said. He wriggled out of my grasp and jumped to the ground, walking beside her as she headed across the parking lot.

I slid onto the passenger seat of Liz's car. "What's up?" I asked.

Tight lines pulled at the corners of her eyes. "I don't have all the details yet but it looks like you and Channing were right. Wilson was mishandling the finances for the camp. More than we already knew."

"I'm sorry," I said. I wasn't surprised but I was sorry.

"So am I," she said. "When I'm not thinking about how I'd like to throttle him."

I reached over and caught one of her hands, giving it a squeeze. "How bad is it?"

"Bad enough. Channing thinks he was showing—on paper—that furniture and appliances were being replaced. But it seems they weren't. There are receipts from a crony of his who was in the furniture business for purchases that weren't made. It's looking like Wilson was taking a kickback. This 'friend' of my brother supplied the nonexistent furniture and appliances at a discount and donated some things outright for a tax break." She stared out the window and we sat in silence for a moment. "Channing is finding a forensic accountant and we'll work with the IRS and whoever else needs to be involved."

She looked at me then. "It will be a while before we can clean out that building. Which means it will be a while before we can start on the health center. As far as I can tell, everything in there was just junk dumped there to make their scheme look real."

I could see the pain in her eyes and hear it in her voice. I thought about something Charlotte had said about Wilson: *More than once I've had the urge to cold-cock Wilson with my soup pot for the grief he's caused Liz.*

Right at that moment I felt the same way. I settled for giving Liz a hug.

When I got inside there was no sign of Charlotte or Elvis but Mac was waiting with coffee for me. "Will you be okay without me for a little while?" he asked. "I'd like to get those stools to the scrap metal recycler."

"You're being a very gracious not-winner," I said.

He laughed. "I like your choice of words."

"As you can see, I am a very gracious *winner*." I held out one hand, palm up.

"Your magnanimity is duly noted," he said.

I smiled and took a sip of my coffee. "Go whenever it works for you. Charlotte and I can handle things here."

Mac went out to the workshop. Charlotte came down the stairs tying her apron and trailed by Elvis.

"I talked to Clayton last night," she said, frowning at the floor by the front entrance. "He thinks there are members of the Phillips family still alive."

"Does he know where they're living?"

"Maybe a place Alfred could start looking. Clayton said his grandmother talked about the family moving to Portland and then to Portsmouth. His grandmother also claimed that Captain Phillips's sister had a child out of wedlock."

"So one more generation."

Charlotte nodded. "Yes. It seems the young woman was sent away. She was supposedly married after a whirlwind romance and then suddenly and sadly widowed with a child. Just over a year later she was back with her family."

"I take it Clayton was a little skeptical about the marriage and widowhood."

"His grandmother certainly was and according to him she always knew the gossip so he thinks she was probably right."

I linked my fingers together and rested my hands on the top of my head. "Do you think finding someone from that family will help find Mark Steele's killer?"

Charlotte considered the question for a moment before she answered. "I don't know. What I do know is that our job is to find information and use it to get to the truth. Who knows which fact will help do that?"

Charlotte and I decided the entryway floor needed to be cleaned before we opened. She ran the vacuum over the space and I wielded the mop.

There were two women waiting when I unlocked the front door. They were looking for a tablecloth for an upcoming dinner party. They left with a cream linen tablecloth, a set of pewter napkin rings and twelve wineglasses. Those two customers were followed by a man looking for a bed frame. We had nothing set up in the shop but I remembered that Mac had been working on a headboard and footboard before the stools had claimed his attention. Only the headboard had been painted, but as soon as the customer saw it he wanted the whole thing and happily put down a deposit.

Mr. P. arrived shortly after that. "I have some security camera footage from a house across the street from Strathmore Inn," he said. "When you have a few spare minutes I'd like to show it to you."

"Go right now," Charlotte said. "If I need you I'll come get you." She gestured at Elvis, who was sitting on a child's rocking chair by the cash desk. "And it's not like I don't have any help."

Mr. P. and I went out to the Angels' sunporch office. He hung up his jacket and took his laptop out of his bag.

The footage from the security camera was of better quality than I'd expected. We could clearly see the person talking to Mark Steele. As Rosalie had said the man was shorter than Mr. Steele. He was wearing a dark jacket and a ball cap. It was impossible to see his face.

I stared at the screen, rubbing my arm with the other hand.

"What is it?" Mr. P. asked.

"I'm not sure," I said slowly. I pointed at the laptop. "Does that look like a Patriots jacket to you? The color and the trim are right."

He leaned in for a closer look. After a moment he nodded. "I think you're correct. That may be helpful."

"I wonder if I could have seen that man somewhere in town. There's something familiar about him as he walks away but I can't figure out what."

"Give it time," he said, patting my arm. "In the meantime, I'll keep digging."

Rose arrived at lunchtime with Avery. I stood in the doorway of the Angels' office as she took off her coat. "I've been thinking that we need to take a closer look at some of the people who were on the show recently," she said.

"Great minds think alike."

She smiled. "That's better than fools seldom differ."

We agreed to split the ten episodes from the past season, watch five each and compare notes.

Mac was out in the workshop doing a light sanding of the footboard from the bed we'd taken the deposit on. At the moment it was pea soup green. "Are you up for an exciting night of watching fake ghosts in creepy, not really haunted houses?" I asked.

"Are you going to be there?" he asked.

"I am," I said.

"Will you be cowering in the shelter of my strong, manly arms?"

"That could probably be arranged."

"Will there be pizza?"

I nodded. "There will."

Mac grinned. "I'm in."

"Could I borrow those strong, manly arms to move a table from the workroom into the shop?" I asked.

"You can." He got to his feet, brushing the dust off of his hands. "Wanna feel my muscles?" he asked, walking backward and flexing his arms in a body-builder pose.

"No, that's okay," I said, struggling not to laugh.

He put his left arm almost in my face and made the bicep twitch somehow. "C'mon. Touch it. You know you want to."

"How much coffee have you had this morning?" I asked. "Because I think you need to switch to decaf. Or one of Avery's smoothies."

"I have not had too much coffee," he said. "I'm just full of the joy of life."

I shook my head. "You're full of something."

He leaned down and kissed me before opening the back door. He was silly this morning. And it wasn't the first time. Mac was a positive person by nature but being able to finally work on his boat was making him happy in a way I hadn't seen before.

We moved the large oval table into the shop and Mac went back out to work on the footboard, pausing in the doorway for one last muscular pose.

"It's all yours," I said to Avery. She had a good eye for color, and I was looking forward to seeing how she'd dress the table. "You can do whatever you want but try to keep with a spring theme."

"Do I have to use all pastel colors?" she asked as she stood back and surveyed the table, tapping on her chin with a closed fist.

"You don't have to use any pastel colors if you don't want to."

She smiled and I knew an idea was already percolating in that creative brain of hers.

I spent the next couple of hours working on my table out in the workshop while Mac finished sanding the rest of the bed frame and then began gluing all the loose joints. When I went back inside, Avery had finished the table. It looked spectacular.

The first thing she had done was surround the table with six chairs from my orphan chair collection—three sets of two matching chairs. "So there's a pattern. So it doesn't look like you just have a bunch of random chairs sitting around," she explained.

She used a lime green tablecloth with blue and white cloth napkins on the table. The napkins were from a mystery box I'd bought at the end of an auction for five dollars. I'd already make more than ten times that much on the contents so far. Avery chose a set of plain white dishes with flowered charger plates. Like the chairs the wineglasses were three sets of two that matched. The cutlery was real silver. It had been in the shop pretty much since we'd opened. No one seemed interested in actual silverware these days. It did look beautiful on the table and I was hoping that showcased like this it would sell. When Avery styled a table we often sold everything on it along with the piece of furniture. And sometimes without it.

She had added tiny paper flowers to each napkin and in the center of the table arranged a collection of milk pitchers holding more paper flowers along with a faux tiny topiary, which also came from the auction box.

"It's perfect," I said.

"It's okay that I brought the chairs out?" Everyone knew about my love for odd chairs. As fast as we sold one I'd somehow stumble on another that needed a little makeover.

"Yes. They do work with that table."

"Maybe if someone buys the table they'll buy the chairs, too." She poked me in the arm with her elbow. "You know, Sarah, the chairs need their own homes where they will be happy. It's not fair to make them live their lives in the workroom."

I stuck my tongue out at her and she laughed. Then she straightened the chair in front of her, moving it maybe half an inch to the right. She turned to look at me again. "You're coming to dinner at Charlotte's on Sunday, right?"

"Absolutely."

She twisted a couple of bracelets around her wrist and shifted from one foot to the other. "I kind of said I would do the table so can I borrow some stuff from here?"

"Sure," I said.

"I'll bring everything back washed."

I nodded. "I know you will."

"And I'll make sure nothing gets broken."

She was nervous about something. She wasn't usually so twitchy. "Avery, I already said yes. What's going on?"

She took a breath and let it out in one rush of air. "Greg and I are . . . I don't know what we are. We've been talking a lot the past couple of weeks and maybe something is happening again and maybe I'm just imagining it but I was thinking of asking Charlotte if I could bring him but I know she'll say yes and maybe it's a bad idea."

It took me a second to make sense out of her run-on sentence. Avery and Greg Pearson had gone out, broken up for some reason she hadn't shared and now it seemed they might be getting back together.

"I vote for inviting him," I said. "He knows us all so that part won't be embarrassing."

She rolled her eyes. "You watch. Nonna will ask him what his intentions are."

I stifled the urge to laugh. "She already did that, remember? And he got massive brownie points when he said he wanted to become a marine biologist and work on ways to clean up the ocean."

"He really does want to be a marine biologist," she said.

I nodded. "I know, because after he said that, he and Mr. P. spent half an hour talking about microplastics in the water system." I smiled. "Invite Greg. Tell him if he doesn't want to come that's okay, too. And if any of them start giving him the third degree I'll swoop in and start talking about . . . about . . ."

"Chairs?" she finished, a tiny smile tugging at her mouth.

I squared my shoulders. "Yes. I will start talking about chairs."

To my surprise she flung her arms around me in a quick, hard hug. "Thank you," she whispered and then before I could say anything she was gone into the workroom.

Mac and I had pizza and a salad I made with carrots, arugula and sprouts he had gotten from the farmers market. Then we curled up to watch *Night Moves*, me with my head on Mac's chest and Elvis sprawled over both of us.

Mark Steele was a charismatic host and I quickly understood why the show had a following. He reminded me a little of actor George Clooney with his thick hair, strong jaw and mischievous boy-next-door smile. He was dressed in jeans and a pale blue button-down shirt, expensive casual clothes like the ones he'd been wearing when he died.

"Is it just me or does he fall over the line from confident to arrogant?" I asked Mac after we'd watched five minutes of the program.

Mad shook his head. "It's not just you."

As I'd told Mr. P., I didn't believe in ghosts, spirits or hauntings. But I tried to be accepting that there were people that did and it didn't mean they were stupid. I knew some of the people on *Night Moves* were con artists and they deserved to be exposed. But others just wanted to believe in possibilities that couldn't be explained by science or logic. I didn't think that was wrong.

"Look at him," I said to Mac, lifting my head from his chest. "Right now. Look at him."

He frowned. "What am I supposed to be seeing?"

I gestured at the TV with one hand. "Look at how he stands. See how he plants his feet apart and gestures with his hands so he takes up more space? Laurel is basically in the background and she's his co-host."

Mac studied the screen for a moment. "You're right," he said.

Meanwhile Mark was talking to a homeowner. "You didn't question that?" he said to her. He was easily a couple of inches over six feet and he seemed to loom over the woman, who was probably a foot shorter. There was also an undertone of condescension in his voice that left me with the feeling that he thought she was stupid.

"That's the second time he's asked that," I said to Mac.

"Third, actually," he said. Elvis meowed his agreement.

I leaned back against him. "Not a vote in the man's favor."

A moment later Mac tapped my arm. "Watch Steele right now. He'll cut off Laurel or talk over her or both."

Laurel Prescott was pointing at two large, multi-paned windows in an upstairs bedroom in the old house they were investigating for two possible ghost encounters. "The reason you noticed the curtain move is because the windows are old and there's a gap between the frame and the sash," she explained.

"The cold air coming in makes the curtains move because—"

"—What Laurel is trying to say is your restless spirit is just a drafty window," Mark finished.

Laurel's eyes narrowed, just slightly. She gave him a tight smile and said, "That's right, Mark."

"I see what you mean," I said.

By the time we'd started on the second episode I'd learned that Mark Steele's two favorite expressions seemed to be "You didn't question that?" and "That made sense to you?"

There were moments when he seemed kinder, for instance when he explained to an eight-year-old boy that there was no ghost in his bedroom closet. What there was was a family of racoons living in the attic above the closet. "They're all moving to a nice den in the woods that they don't have to share with people," Mark had explained. But those moments were rare.

Mac kept his phone handy and did a quick online search for the woman who was featured in the first episode.

"She can't be the killer," he said. "She's in jail for fraud unrelated to her so-called haunted cottage."

The man in the second episode was also a bust. It turned out he was living in Costa Rica, where he owned a small hotel. "Big surprise," Mac said. "It's haunted."

The owner of the haunted house in the third episode was a man named Steve Suzuki. His claim that his home was haunted by the ghost of a murdered man was debunked pretty quickly. Standing in the middle of his office he tried to explain away what he'd done as just entertainment, a little harmless fun, while still insisting there was a ghost in his home. Over his left shoulder I caught a brief glimpse of a framed Rob Gronkowski football jersey. I sat up, annoying Elvis, and stared at the screen. "Go back," I said to Mac, gesturing over my shoulder.

He rewound the interview. It was definitely a Patriots jersey with the tight end's number eighty-seven I'd spotted, which meant Steve Suzuki was a Patriots fan.

"It's him," I said. I turned to look at Mac and a still annoyed Elvis.

He looked confused. "That guy killed Mark Steele? How do you know?"

I shook my head. "No, no, no. He's not the killer although he might be." I stood up. "I need to talk to Mr. P."

I went down the hall and knocked on Rose's door. "Is Mr. P. here?" I asked when she opened the door.

"Yes, Alfred is here," she said. "Come in."

It turned out Mr. P. was having a facial and his face was covered with a creamy blue mask. I tried not to focus on the fact that it made him look like a Smurf.

"Mac and I were watching one of the episodes of *Night Moves*," I said. "The owner of the haunted house that was featured, his name is Steve Suzuki, is the man who was talking to Mark Steele in the parking lot the day Steele was killed."

"What makes you so sure?" Mr. P. asked.

Mac was standing in the doorway now.

"He had Gronk's jersey on his office wall."

"I'm sorry, I'm not following," Mr. P. said.

"Remember when we were looking at the video of

the man talking to Mark Steele and I said it looked like he was wearing a New England Patriots jacket? Now I'm certain he was. But it's an older-style Patriots jacket. Dad has one. Steve Suzuki is the only Patriots fan we've encountered so far in this case. Only a long-time fan would have one of those jackets."

"Is that the jacket that your mother keeps saying she hoped didn't accidentally fall under the snow blower?" Rose asked.

I nodded. "That's the one."

She looked at Mr. P. "I've seen Peter in the jacket Sarah is talking about. It's navy blue with gray on the shoulders and the arms and the team logo on one front side."

"But no logo on the back," I said.

She nodded.

"It's him. I know it's him," I said.

"Then we need to find Mr. Suzuki," Mr. P. said.

Rose patted his arm. "Easy peasy," she said.

Chapter 14

It turned out it *was* easy peasy to find Steve Suzuki. The past season of *Night Moves* had been set in New England and his house was in Rockport. A quick search on his laptop and Mr. P. had the address.

"That wasn't even a challenge," he said, pushing his glasses up his nose.

"We'll try to make it harder for you next time," I teased.

We decided we'd leave midmorning on Sunday so we'd be back in lots of time for dinner at Charlotte's. "So what's the plan?" I asked Rose. She was hanging several woolen blankets on a wooden quilt rack.

"We're going to talk to Mr. Suzuki," she said, her tone suggesting that was obvious.

"I know that," I said. "But we're not going to just go knock on his door and then when he answers ask if he killed Mark Steele."

"Why not?" She leaned back, giving the blankets a critical look. Then she switched two of them around.

"So just ambush the man?"

"I don't think 'ambush' is the right word. I think 'catch him unawares' is a better description."

I opened my mouth to explain that might backfire and then closed it again. Arguing with Rose was like arguing with Elvis. I was never going to win. At best I'd be humored and both of them would do what they'd always intended to do. At worst I'd be ignored and they would do what they'd intended to do.

Mac left early to make the lasagna. He put two cloth grocery bags in his truck, which I took as a very good sign.

I spent the afternoon sanding the top of the farmhouse table. It was going to look terrific once I'd finished painting the legs and varnishing the top.

I could smell the lasagna when we stepped into the hallway. Elvis looked at me and licked his whiskers. "You're a cat," I told him. "Cats eat cat food, not lasagna."

He gave me the stink eye and swished his tail through the air.

I let myself into the apartment to find Mac washing dishes and singing along to the *Hamilton* soundtrack.

"That smells incredible," I said, putting my arms around his waist.

"I hope it tastes as good," he said.

I kissed his ear. "Your lasagna has never disappointed me."

And it didn't this time, either.

Rose did supply the brownies and Mac sent her back to her apartment with two servings of the lasagna. "If you like it, I'll give Alfred the recipe," he said.

We headed for Rockport before lunch the next morning. Steve Suzuki's house was easy to find. It was a traditional colonial style, two story, painted a gray-green with white trim and a red shingled roof. The same number of small, multipaned windows were spaced on either side of and above the front door. The house sat on a beautifully landscaped lot.

We found Mr. Suzuki in his yard and Mr. P. introduced us and explained about being hired by Delia Watson.

"Are you here to ask if I killed Mark Steele?" he asked. He was about five-ten or so with black hair under a Patriots ball cap.

"Did you?" Rose asked. Then she gave him her best sweet grandma smile. "It would certainly make things go easier for us."

He smiled. "I'm sorry to make things more difficult for you, but no, I didn't. I hated him, that's no secret. Because of Mark Steele and his TV show I almost had to declare bankruptcy."

"Almost?" Mr. P. said.

Suzuki swiped a hand over his mouth. "My father-in-law bailed us out, which believe me isn't a position I want to be in. I was a little overextended. There were several people interested in the house but all of that interest disappeared after the episode aired."

"Mr. Suzuki, why did you agree to do the show—why does anyone?" I asked. That question had been bothering me since the first episode I'd watched.

"Have you seen *Night Moves*?" he said.

I nodded.

"Just the past season or earlier ones?"

"Just the most recent one."

"Go look at a couple of episodes from the first two seasons. *Night Moves* was less of an attack show then. Sometimes Mark and Laurel and the team couldn't come up with a rational explanation for what they experienced. Sometimes it was left to the viewers to work out what was real. *That's* why I agreed to do the show. That's why a lot of people did, I suspect." He shrugged.

"You spoke to Mr. Steele the day he died," Mr. P. said.

Suzuki nodded. "Yeah, I did. A friend of mine saw him in North Harbor. Told me he was staying at the Strathmore Inn. I drove up there, waited around and when I saw him come out I confronted him in the parking lot."

"And what did you want from him?" Mr. P. said.

Suzuki pulled off his ball cap and squeezed the bill with one hand. "I wanted them to reedit the episode and show some of the things they cut that did suggest the house was haunted. It is. I wasn't making that up."

Rose and I exchanged a look. "You claimed the spirit of a murdered man was haunting this house," she said. "Your alleged ghost hadn't been murdered at all. He'd lived to the ripe old age of ninety-two and died in his sleep."

A flush of color flooded his face. "So I embellished a little. But there was—*there is* a ghost. What Mark Steele did wasn't fair."

"What did he say when you talked to him?" Mr. P. asked.

Suzuki shook his head. "He said I deserved what I got. The guy was a jerk and I told him that. Then I said his day was coming." He sighed. "I wish I hadn't said that last part."

Rose gave him a sympathetic smile. And I knew she was sympathetic, not just trying to play the man so he might reveal more than he intended to. She had a very forgiving heart. "What did you do after you talked to Mr. Steele?" she said.

"I spent close to two hours at a pub down by the waterfront. I had a cup of coffee and then I ended up ordering lunch." He was still holding the ball cap. He seemed twitchy all of a sudden, as though he had something to hide. Or maybe it was Rose's steady gray eyes locked on his face. That gaze had made me twitchy a time or two.

"Can anyone vouch for you?"

He swallowed and ran his free hand over his neck. "You have to understand the position Steele left me in. I know all about turning the other cheek but I just couldn't let the man get away with what he'd done."

Rose continued to look at him, head cocked to one side, no judgment, just curiosity.

Steve looked away and then his gaze came back to Rose. "I was meeting with a woman who had known Steele back in his college days. Her name is Gemini Elderberry. And I doubt that's her real name. She's a psychic who Steele briefly worked with when he was a broke college student years ago. The guy worked for a psychic. There had to be something there, right?"

He stopped playing with his hat and put it back on. "I found out about her in an online chat room where people get together to crap on the show. So I contacted her. It turned out she's here in Maine with five or six other psychics and they're giving readings around the state. She said she could meet me on Sunday and when I found out Steele was in North Harbor as well, I thought maybe things were going to turn around for me."

"So you were with Ms. Elderberry from the time you left the Strathmore Inn until what time?" Mr. P. asked.

Steve shifted uneasily from one foot to the other. "I wasn't with her all the time. I headed for the pub right after I left the inn but she was late. It was about one o'clock before she showed up. She said she made a wrong turn and got lost. The whole thing turned out to be a bust. It turned out all Steele did was sell tickets at the door and T-shirts at intermission."

"Do you remember the name of the place?" I asked. I had a feeling I already knew the answer.

"Something to do with bears. The Brown Bear or the Bear's Den maybe?"

"The Black Bear," I said.

He nodded. "Yeah, that's it. I think they would remember me. It wasn't that busy."

Steve gave Gemini Elderberry's contact information to Mr. P. and we got back in my SUV. "I'll talk to

Sammy and check Mr. Suzuki's alibi but I think we can cross him off our list." Mr. P. said.

"I think we should talk to this Gemini Elderberry," Rose said. "It wouldn't hurt to learn more about Mr. Steele's past."

I dropped Rose at Charlotte's house and Mr. P. at his apartment with a promise that I'd pick him up later for dinner. When I got home I found Elvis flopped at the top of his cat tower with his legs hanging over the side. He looked very relaxed. "I think I'm going to be a cat in my next life," I said.

He opened one green eye, looked at me and then closed it again. I made a chicken sandwich with the last of the arugula and sprouts and decided to watch another episode of *Night Moves*. I very quickly eliminated the couple involved. They seemed to have capitalized on having been on the program and accused of faking their ghost. A quick online search showed me that they were doing more business than they were before. It didn't seem like they'd had any reason to kill Mark Steele.

I remembered what Steve Suzuki had said about the early seasons of *Night Moves* and decided to watch a show from the first year. He was right. The episode was less confrontational than the episodes I'd seen from this last season and Mark seemed less condescending. There were also more details about the history of the house and the families that had lived in it. I thought the program was a lot more interesting. I wondered what prompted the change and suspected it was because controversy and confrontation seem to sell.

Elvis had decided that draping himself across my legs and mooching chicken was more fun than lounging on his cat tower. I checked the time and then picked him up and set him on the floor. "Get cleaned up," I said. "We're leaving in fifteen minutes."

He stretched and began to wash his face. I stood up, stretched and went to wash mine. Charlotte had insisted I bring Elvis. "He's part of the family," she'd said. "You can't leave him home all by himself."

When I came out of the bedroom he was waiting by the front door. "You're very punctual," I said as I pulled on my jacket.

He followed me out and settled himself on the front seat of the car. "We're going to get Jess first," I said.

Elvis gave a mrrr of approval. He liked Jess. She talked to him as though he were a person and snuck him treats when she thought I wasn't looking.

"Hey, Elvis! How's it shakin'?" Jess said as she slid onto the passenger seat. Right on cue the cat meowed and shook his head. I wasn't sure if it was her who had trained Elvis or the cat that had trained her.

Mr. P. was waiting for us on the sidewalk. Much like Elvis he was ready on time or more likely a little bit early. We headed for Charlotte's house and Mr. P. and Jess talked about vegetarian food while Elvis looked on with what seemed to me to be a very skeptical expression. Mr. P. had been to the new vegetarian restaurant that had opened a couple of weeks ago. Jess wanted to try it. "So are you coming with me?" she said.

I shrugged. "All right." From the corner of my eye I could see her staring at me, mouth hanging open a little.

"'All right' as in 'yes'? Or 'all right' as in you'll stall until I stop asking, which for the record I will not do."

"The first one," I said.

She turned just her head and looked at Mr. P. in the backseat. "Try to act normal," she stage-whispered. "Sarah has been abducted by aliens and one of them has taken her place."

"I must say I'm impressed by their attention to detail," Mr. P. said, playing right along. "The skin and hair look very human-like."

Elvis meowed his agreement. He didn't want to be left out of the conversation.

"All three of you are hilarious," I said. "And I'm serious. I'm game to try that vegetarian place."

Jess looked at Mr. P. again. "I vote for keeping this Sarah," she said.

We spent the rest of the drive discussing all the ways to cook with chickpeas.

"Something smells delicious," I said when Charlotte opened the door. I fervently hoped there were no chickpeas involved.

"Beef stew and dumplings with apple crisp for dessert," she said.

My stomach growled in appreciation.

I set Elvis down and he wandered around, stopping to say hello to everyone before settling in next to Liz. No one asked why I'd brought my cat.

"I can move him," I said to Liz.

She waved me with away with one hand. "Leave him be. He's a great conversationalist."

The cat gave me a smug little smile.

Charlotte had unearthed Nick's old rod hockey game and he and Greg were playing each other. Avery was tweaking the table setting. She had used a striped white and blue cloth with crisp white napkins, each tied with a pink ribbon and a detailed paper-cut leaf, plus Charlotte's blue dishes. The water glasses were a vibrant fuchsia set that I recognized from the shop. There were several chubby, pink pillar candles spread down the center length of the table interspersed with small bowls, each with several pink, floating daisies.

I smiled at Avery. "It's beautiful, warm and welcoming and not fussy."

"Thank you," she said. She glanced across the room. "Thanks for pushing me to invite Greg. I think he's having fun."

I followed her gaze. "I think he's waxing Nick's backside."

The rod hockey game had drawn a crowd—Jess, Mr. P., Mac and Rose, who all seemed to be cheering for Greg. I knew Nick was good at the game. We had played it a lot as kids.

I went into the kitchen to see if I could help Charlotte.

"Everything is done," she said, "but thank you for asking. The stew is in the oven and the apple crisp is about to join it."

I leaned against the counter and watched her slide

a giant casserole dish into the oven. "It was great idea to bring out the hockey game," I said.

Charlotte smiled. "I was cleaning out some boxes from the basement and there it was. I'd been thinking of getting you to stick it in the shop—no one uses it anymore." She inclined her head in the direction of the living room, where a loud cheer had just erupted. "But now I think I'll keep it."

She turned to hang up her oven mitts.

"Who are we waiting for?" I asked. I'd noticed that Avery had set two more places at the table than we had people at the moment.

"Your grandmother and Michelle," Charlotte said.

"I could have brought Gram."

"I know." She opened the cupboard door next to me and reached for her glass dessert bowls.

"I'll get those," I said. I lifted the dishes down from the shelf and set them on the counter.

"Thank you," she said. "Isabel is a very last-minute addition. You know John has been in New Hampshire for the last week filing in for a former colleague at UNH."

I nodded. Gram's second husband, John Scott, was a retired history professor. He was tall with brown hair flecked with gray and an angular face. John was thirteen years younger than Gram was, which had raised a lot of eyebrows when they had started seeing each other, not that Gram "cared a fig," as she put it, about what anyone thought.

"He was supposed to be home today."

"He was," Charlotte said. "But it turns out they

need him for an extra couple of days so I told Isabel she had to come. We have more than enough food. Michelle was coming anyway and she said she'd be happy to pick her up." She glanced at her watch. "They should be here anytime now."

"Thank you for inviting Michelle," I said. "She has no family here anymore."

"Yes she does," Charlotte said. "She has us." I laid my head on her shoulder for a moment and she patted my cheek.

There was a knock at the back door then. Gram and Michelle had arrived. My grandmother wrapped me in a big hug. "It's so good to see you," she said. "I was talking to your brother right before Michelle picked me up." Isabel Grayson Scott was about five foot seven or so and her lovely posture made her seem taller. She had deep blue eyes and wavy white hair she wore cropped short. Her smooth, creamy skin, gorgeous cheekbones and long neck meant she was often mistaken for being younger than she was. And she was one of those people who was as beautiful on the inside as she was on the outside.

One of the many things I loved about my grandmother was how welcoming she had been to Liam and my stepdad, Peter. If she minded that Peter had filled the role of father for me after my father died, she never showed it. And she was as much Liam's grandmother as she was mine. Since Liam's biological grandparents were all dead she was the only grandparent he had. He loved her just as much as I did and I knew Gram adored him.

"Is he still working on that tiny house project?" I asked as I took Gram's coat.

She nodded. "He is but he should wrap things up in a couple of weeks and then he's coming here for a while. And he said to tell you he'll call you tonight."

Liam was a building contractor and a very skilled carpenter. He'd worked on building tiny houses for a while and then gone back to renovating old houses, which was where his heart really was, but he'd agreed to help with a tiny house project in New Hampshire that was going provide places to live for people who right now were on the street.

"I'm glad he's coming. I'm trying to convince him to move here. I don't see why he couldn't use North Harbor as his base of operations."

Gram smiled. "I'd like that. We may have to work together on that."

I turned to Michelle. "I'm so glad you came," I said.

"Me too," she said.

Michelle and Gram had each brought a bottle of nonalcoholic sparkling wine, the same nonalcoholic wine we'd used in the picnic baskets.

I helped Avery find enough wineglasses and was then dismissed while she rearranged the table a bit. I took the glasses Avery didn't want back to the kitchen and then bent down to peek in the oven. Charlotte swatted me with an oven mitt. "Don't even think about opening that oven door," she warned.

"I wasn't," I said, hanging my head.

She pointed toward the living room. "Go," she said.

I went.

Nick was now playing Liz, who was being coached by Greg with a bit of help from Elvis. There was some trash talk going on. Liz called Nick a pretty boy. He suggested her reflexes were slow. I saw the gleam in her eye. "Does he have a death wish?" I whispered to Rose, who was standing beside me.

"Even worse," she said. "He has his mother's competitive streak."

"Charlotte's not competitive," I said.

"Play poker with her sometime and see if you still say that," Rose retorted.

I frowned. "Charlotte plays poker? For money?"

Rose patted my cheek. "I just said that, sweetie. Try to keep up."

It was a close game but in the end Liz was victorious. She was all graciousness, smiling at Nick and thanking him for a good game. Their wager seemed to have been designed for maximum embarrassment. Before we ate, Nick had to recite "I'm a Little Teapot" complete with actions. I didn't even try not to laugh. When he finished he pointed a finger at Liz. "You are going down, old woman," he said, narrowing his eyes at her.

She made a *come to me* gesture with one hand. "Any time, pretty boy. Any time." Then she turned and high-fived Greg. He smiled back at her, cheeks turning pink. Happiness was written all over Avery's face.

Supper was delicious. Avery and Greg cleared the table. Mac made more tea. I caught him in the kitchen and threaded my fingers through his. "You and Michelle are in charge of entertainment."

"There's entertainment?" he said.

I nodded. "Nick found a bunch of old home movies in the garage. He had them digitized." I handed him a thumb drive. "Mr. P. will set things up for you. Jess and Nick and I will do the dishes."

No surprise Charlotte objected to being put out of her own kitchen. "Sit," Nick said, pointing toward the living room.

"You're a very bossy child," she said, hands on her hips.

"Wonder where I learned that?" he said, raising an eyebrow at her.

I washed the glasses and pots, Nick dried and Jess loaded everything else into the dishwasher. We made short work of it all. "Thanks, guys," Nick said.

We joined the others to find Avery and Greg collapsed in laughter at the sight of Isabel, Rose, Charlotte and Liz dressed as the Spice Girls at what looked like some kind of fundraiser.

"Wait a minute, who's Ginger Spice?" I asked, trying to figure out who the fifth group member was.

"Oh, that's Maddie Hamilton," Gram said. "It was a fundraiser for the school hot lunch program."

Maddie, as Ginger Spice, wore a blond wig with a one-shouldered silver sequined top and matching shorts along with very high silver sandals. Liz was Posh Spice. Her wig was an exact replica of Victoria Beckham's angular bob. She wore a sparkly, silver, thin-strapped, cleavage-revealing top over matching leggings and a pair of silver sandals with heels so high they would have given me a nosebleed. She had Beckham's pout down perfectly. Scary Spice was

Charlotte decked out in a white, body-hugging, halter-neck jumpsuit sprinkled with rhinestones, a long black curly wig and knee-high silver boots.

Jess looked over at Charlotte and gave her a thumbs-up. "You were hot!"

Charlotte blushed a little. "Thank you," she said.

Gram was Sporty Spice in white jeans with an enormous silver belt, a lacy, white and silver sleeveless cropped top and a white jacket trimmed with faux ostrich feathers, a dark wig covering her hair.

Baby Spice was Rose, of course, in a blond wig, a white and silver baby doll dress and silver platform heels. I saw Mr. P. catch her eye and wink.

In the video they were lip-synching to "Wannabe." I thought they were fantastic.

Mac held up his hands and clapped. Michelle gave a wolf whistle. I expected Avery to be mortified but she was looking at her grandmother with what seemed to be admiration.

"I vote for a reunion performance," Jess said.

Three voices firmly said no and one said maybe. The maybe was Rose.

"Why not?" she said. "I'm old, not dead. And I still fit into that dress." And then she winked at Mr. P.

We moved on to teenage Nick playing guitar and singing, and Gram pointed out his hair was pretty much a mullet. I leaned against Liz. "I remember when Charlotte bought the rod hockey game," I said quietly.

"It wasn't yesterday," Liz said.

"I remember how much Nick and I played and how much you and Charlotte did. You were really good."

"That was a long time ago."

I nodded. "Yes, it was. You were lucky you had Greg to coach you today."

Liz had always had a great poker face. "Yes, I was," she said.

I kissed her cheek. "Love you," I said.

She smiled then and I knew what was coming. "Yeah, yeah," she said. "Everyone does."

Chapter 15

It was not a quiet Monday morning at Second Chance. There were more web orders than usual. A dozen people in two SUVs—all from the same family—stopped in on their way from Rockport heading home to New Brunswick and two different B and B owners showed up with long lists of things they needed.

The table Avery had dressed had sold, complete with the chairs and everything she had set it with. Charlotte and I carefully packed the table settings in two boxes and Mac helped the buyer pad the table and chairs and get them settled in the back of his half-ton. Luckily the man had brought a bunch of moving blankets with him.

By the time we packed a beautiful set of china and cutlery for the second B and B owner I was feeling hungry. It was almost noon. And I had forgotten to bring my lunch. It was still in the refrigerator at home. "This is your fault," I said to Elvis, who was perched inside the one cardboard box we hadn't used. He had been sprawled on his cat tower when it was time to leave, and after sweeping hand gestures and four *let's go*'s hadn't worked I'd had to pick him up, which was probably what his intention had been all along. I pointed a finger at him. "You owe me lunch."

"Why don't you go to Glenn's?" Charlotte said. "I think he lets Elvis run a tab."

"Good idea," I said. "Can I bring you anything back? I mean since Elvis is buying."

"I'd love a lemon tart if they have any," she said. She smiled at the cat. "Thank you, Elvis."

The line was several people deep when I got to Mc-Namara's but Glenn kept things moving. I ordered a ham and cheddar sandwich with mustard and dill pickles and three lemon tarts, one for Charlotte, one for me and one for Liz because they were her favorite. "Perfect timing," Glenn said as he put the tarts in a small cardboard box. "These are the last three."

He was a big man, over six feet with broad shoulders and huge hands. He still wore his blond hair in the brush cut he'd had when he played football in college.

"My dad says perfect timing is the key to a happy life."

"I thought comfortable shoes were the key to a happy life."

"That too," I said.

The crush of people had disappeared. "I heard you were the one who found the TV guy at Gladstone House," Glenn said.

"Michelle and me, actually."

"He was in here, more than once."

I nodded. "I know. I saw him in here the Friday before he died. Did you talk to him at all?"

"I gave him directions to the historical society," he said. "And he asked me where we get our coffee beans. Very intense man."

There was a stack of flyers on the counter by the cash register. They were advertising the Connections Tour, the group of psychics coming to the Halloran Arena complex. I scanned the list of participating psychics and mediums. Gemini Elderberry was one of them.

"Do you believe in this kind of thing?" I asked Glenn, holding up one of the flyers.

He laughed. "No. Dealing with people I can see and hear is quite enough for me, thank you very much. But I did go to a show last year in Rockport with a medium slash hypnotist and that was a lot of fun."

My sandwich was ready then. I grabbed my food and one of the flyers. "Have a good afternoon," Glenn said.

"Yeah, you too," I said. I turned around and almost walked into Emily Hastings.

"I'm sorry, Sarah," she said. "I was trying to figure out what kind of sandwich I wanted and I wasn't watching where I was going."

"It's okay. No harm done," I said. I held up the bag with my sandwich. "I can recommend the ham and cheese."

"That does sound good," she said. "Usually I'm trying to supervise twenty kids and grab a bite in between keeping them in their seats and making sure *they* all actually eat something." I'd seen Emily helping serve lunch as part of the hot lunch program at the elementary school. She had a smile and a kind word for everyone.

The smile faded from her face. "I'm sorry that you had to find Mr. Steele's body."

"I wish I could have done something to help him," I said.

She wore a wide silver Celtic knot ring and she slid it up and down her right ring finger. "I didn't like the man but I didn't want him dead, either. I just wish he could have accepted that we didn't want to be on his show. It didn't seem to matter how many times my grandmother said no. He wouldn't stop asking." A frown creased her forehead and her hazel eyes narrowed. "You know that she had nothing to do with what happened. Gram can't manage the stairs. She hasn't been on the second floor in a least a couple of years."

I nodded. "I know."

"If the car hadn't broken down I guess I'd be a suspect. Gram says it's a good thing it did, but if I'd been there Mr. Steele would never have gotten into the house in the first place." She sighed. "Gladstone House means everything to my grandmother. He just should have let it go."

When I got back to the shop Rose and Mr. P. were in the Angels' office. "Gemini Elderberry might be in town right now," I said, handing her the flyer I'd gotten at Glenn's.

"She is," Rose said. "We're going to meet with her tomorrow morning."

"How are you always one step ahead of me?" I asked.

She lifted her gaze from the flyer. "I'm old. People tend to underestimate me."

I put one hand on my hip. "Rose Jackson, I knew better than to underestimate you when I was six."

She smiled. "You were a very savvy child. And I didn't mean you underestimate me. I mean a lot of other people do. Plus I have ears like a wolf."

I smiled back at her. "True on both accounts. So have you managed to dig up anything on our psychic?"

Rose nodded. "Yes. It was a productive morning. One of my former students works at a casino in Atlantic City. You just know when a young man can count cards and favors fishnet stocking that he's going to do something out of the ordinary with his life. Trevor has connections with a talent booking agent and says that Gemini's real name is Katherine Elder. She's from the West Coast. She's been working as a psychic and hypnotist for more than twenty years. According to Trevor there were accusations that she planted people in the audience at several of her shows a few years ago, and before that, that she used spies to make note of things people said as they were coming in to the venue."

"Those tricks have been around for a long time," Mr. P. said.

"Because they work."

He nodded. "People like Ms. Elderberry use their observational skills to read people."

"Read them how?" I asked.

He pointed at the box I was holding. "Those are lemon tarts."

I shook my head. "Which you know because Charlotte told you she asked me to bring her one. That's luck, not good observational skills."

"Three lemon tarts."

I stared at him for a moment. "Okay," I said. "How do you know that?"

A smile played across his face. "I've noticed that you like lemon tarts as well."

"So why did I buy three and not two?"

"Because they're Elizabeth's favorite and you are a very kind person."

I shook my head. "Alfred Peterson, sometimes you scare me."

He put a hand over his heart. "I promise to only use my powers for the forces of good and never for evil," he said solemnly.

"Good to know," I said. I studied him for a moment. "Would you visit a psychic?"

"I don't believe I would," he said. "I don't see that the dead would need us to spend twenty-nine ninety-five just to say hello from the Great Beyond."

"Would you stay at Gladstone House?"

"Do you mean with the goal of seeing Emmeline's ghost?"

I nodded. "Yes."

"Perhaps," he said with a little shrug. "I confess I am a little curious about the experience."

"So am I," Rose said. Her expression turned thoughtful. "Maybe I can find us a little more information."

The afternoon was not as busy as the morning had been and I spent a good hour sanding my farm table. One more session and it would be ready to paint. Rose came across the parking lot as I was putting the table back in the old garage.

"Do you remember my friend Tabitha?" she asked without preamble.

I nodded. "I remember her," I said. "She had a gorgeous chrome table and chair set in her kitchen."

"She also has a cousin who stayed at Gladstone House. We're having tea with them tomorrow afternoon." She turned to go back to the shop. "Try not to drool over Tabitha's things," she said over her shoulder. "There's no way you're getting your hands on any of it until she's planted."

Mac came for dinner and I made waffles with fruit and cheese. I was still enamored of the little waffle maker that Jess had given me for Christmas. After we ate we watched the remaining episode of *Night Moves*. Once again we eliminated the person featured in the episode from our suspect list. A quick search revealed that the man was dead.

Rose drove in with me in the morning. Apparently Mr. P. was walking because he wanted to get his steps in. We were meeting Gemini at Glenn's at ten o'clock.

Gemini Elderberry was not what I was expecting, probably because my mental image of the woman was pretty stereotypical. I was expecting someone in a flowing peasant skirt with lots of jangly bracelets and maybe a head scarf. Instead the woman waiting for us at a table looked to be in her midforties. She had blond corkscrew curls that just brushed the top of her shoulders and a scattering of freckles across the tops of her cheeks. She was wearing jeans and a white button-down shirt with no bracelets at all. Her only jewelry was a gold locket and a gold signet ring on her right hand.

Mr. P. did the introductions and Rose went to the counter to get tea for herself and coffee for Mr. P. and me.

Gemini Elderberry had a low, husky voice that I imagined could sound very compelling onstage. She verified that she had met Steve Suzuki at The Black Bear but she didn't have anything to tell him that he could use against Mark Steele.

"I'm guessing Steve told you I was late," she said, playing with the cup in front of her. She had long fingers with short, unpolished nails.

"He did," Mr. P. said.

"I really was lost," she said. "That's what I get for relying on GPS instead of just looking at a map. I stopped at a small art gallery outside of Camden and asked for directions. They were just opening. I think they'd remember me."

"Mark Steele did work for you," Rose said, adding a little sugar to her tea.

"He did," she said, "but that was quite a few years ago. He was a broke student looking to make some money. He wasn't with us that long. Just one summer. Mark sold tickets and T-shirts and helped set things up when we needed him."

Rose took a sip of her tea. "Did he spy on people for you?"

Gemini laughed. "Yes, on occasion he did. Back then I was just starting out and I was unsure of my abilities."

"How long have you had these abilities?" Mr. P. asked.

"Always. I knew my grandmother was dead before anyone else because she came and told me she had to leave us. It upset my mother when I told her that Nana was dead but she was fine. But I knew she was. I'd seen her."

"You tried to blackmail Mr. Steele," Mr. P. said. His words surprised me more than they seemed to surprise Gemini.

"Why do you think that?" she said.

"You admitted that he gleaned information from people at your shows, information that you used to convince them you could talk to the dead."

She took a sip of her tea. If she was at all rattled it didn't show. "As I said that happened a long time ago. Before I felt confident in my abilities."

Mr. P. didn't rattle easily, either. "Mr. Steele is a celebrity of sorts thanks to his show. But how would it look if people found out that the ghost debunker used to help scam people?" he said. "And these days people are less interested in the kind of live show you put on."

She smiled. "I was lost, remember. I didn't see Mark the day he died and I didn't kill him." She gripped the edge of the table with both hands and got to her feet. There was a walking cast on her left leg. "I slipped on some ice. My ankle had to be pinned. Stairs are not my friend at the moment."

Rose and Mr. P. exchanged a look.

"I can tell you one thing about Mark," Gemini said as she sat back down. "He didn't like to hear no and he didn't believe in compromise. I think whoever killed him had to be on the opposite side of something he wanted to do."

There wasn't anything more to say. I didn't see how Gemini could be Mark Steele's killer. There was no way she could have navigated the stairs at Gladstone House with that boot on her foot.

As we got up to leave, Gemini looked at Mr. P. and said, "Robbie says he still feels bad about the birdhouse."

He stared at her for a long moment. "Thank you for your time, Ms. Elderberry," he finally said.

We climbed in the SUV. I fastened my seat belt and turned to look at Mr. P. He looked unsettled, lips pulled into a thin line. "What was that about?" I asked.

"Robbie was my brother," he said. He took a breath and let it out slowly. "When we were boys he destroyed a birdhouse I had been working on for a scout badge. It was an accident. He was really sorry about it."

"That was a lucky guess," I said. "Nothing more."

"He could have discovered your brother's name with a little research," Rose said. "And if she learned you were a Boy Scout, the birdhouse comment could have been an educated guess."

"I'm sure you're both right," Mr. P. said but he didn't seem completely convinced.

My phone chimed then. It was a text from Mac. "Delia Watson is at the shop."

"Tell him we're on our way," Mr. P. said.

I glanced at Rose, who gave an almost imperceptible nod. I started the car.

We found Delia in the shop with Charlotte. Delia was holding a cup of coffee and talking about coming up with the idea for *Night Moves*. Charlotte was listening intently, the way she did when anyone talked. It was one of the qualities that had made her such a good principal. She was interested in people and that came out when she talked with them.

Rose and Mr. P. took Delia back to their office and Mr. P. indicated that I should join them.

I'd done a little research online on Delia. Before *Night Moves* she'd worked on a show about animal oddities like fish with legs and bees without stingers. Before that she'd been part of a dating show.

"I'm sorry my timing was off," she said, taking a seat and setting her mug on the table. "I just wanted to get an update. The police aren't telling me anything."

Elvis had padded into the room. He made his way over to Delia and sat at her feet. She smiled down at him, which he took as an invitation to jump onto her lap. I made a move to get him but Rose gave her head a little shake.

"I'm sorry," Mr. P. said. "We don't have a lot to tell you, either. We've eliminated several suspects and there are more people we need to talk to."

Delia shook her head, absently stroking the cat's fur. "I don't understand how Mark could have been in that house and no one heard or saw anything."

"Do you know why he left for Gladstone House so early?" Rose asked.

"I don't." She was a pretty good liar but I noticed how her gaze slid away from Rose's face just a fraction of a second too soon. It was something Mr. P. had taught me to watch for. Not an infallible indicator but useful. Elvis, on the other hand, was a pretty much infallible lie detector, at least when he felt like it. Whether he was reading body language, sensing changes in a person's pulse and respiration or just had some sort of woo-woo ability I didn't know. Right now he had a sour expression on his face. Confirmation that Delia had just told us a lie. None of us had any idea how he did that but it had happened enough times that we knew not to ignore that face.

Rose and Alfred had noticed Elvis as well.

"But you were supposed to go with him," Rose said. "That's what you told us. Why did you want to stand around outdoors waiting to get inside? It wasn't like the line was going to be running around the block once the tour started."

Delia leaned back in the chair. She stared up at the ceiling, one hand still stroking Elvis's head.

"He wanted to take one more shot at persuading Annie to be part of the show," Mr. P. said.

She nodded. "Yeah, he did."

"Why? Why couldn't he let this story go? There must be hundreds of so-called haunted houses in New England."

"Thousands." Delia dropped her gaze to Mr. P. "Mark couldn't let anything go. But it was more than that. He was convinced there was a bigger story here than just what's-her-name and the sea captain and he was determined to find out what it was. He knew the ratings were down and he thought this was a way to bring them back up again."

"So why did he leave without you?" Rose asked. She was holding her cup but hadn't taken a drink.

"We argued. I told him it was a waste of time. Annie Hastings was never going to say yes, if for no other reason than she couldn't stand Mark. I should have gone after him but the truth is, I was sick of his obsession with that damn house."

Mark Steele's obsession with Gladstone House had probably gotten him killed.

"And it wouldn't have saved the show," she continued. "The public's interest in *Night Moves* is waning and the show is likely going to be canceled. I could see the writing on the wall even if Mark couldn't. I know I told you I was dealing with an emergency but that's not exactly true. I called a friend who just got a job at a new streaming service and I bounced an idea off of him for a new show. The camera would follow homeowners while they tried to figure out what was behind the ghostly things happening at their houses."

"Like *Ghostbusters* meets *Survivor*," Mr. P. said.

Delia's face lit up. "Exactly and may I use that pitch?"

"Be my guest," he said.

She picked up her mug and drained the last of her coffee. Then she looked at Mr. P. again. "Mark was my friend. One of the few I have . . . had in this business. In the end what I want more than a new show, more than finding out what the secret is in that old house, is the person who killed my friend to be punished. Please just make that happen."

I looked at Elvis. She'd meant every word.

Mr. P. nodded. "We will."

Chapter 16

Gemma McLaughlin was the polar opposite of her cousin Tabitha, I discovered. Tabitha was just under five feet tall and Gemma was probably five-eight or -nine in her stocking feet. Tabitha's hair was dyed a glow-in-the-dark shade of magenta while her cousin's was snow-white. And Tabitha favored T-shirts and yoga pants while Gemma wore a blue-patterned, long-sleeved dress with sensible flats.

Tabitha made tea and Rose had brought a tin of her black-and-white pinwheel cookies along with some brown sugar fudge which I knew from the last visit we'd made to Tabitha's apartment was her favorite.

We sat at the kitchen table and I resisted the urge to run my hand over the tabletop of her chrome dining set.

"Tabby says you have some questions about Gladstone House," Gemma said.

Rose nodded. "I'm sure Tabitha told you that I'm a private investigator."

"It sounds very exciting." Gemma gave her an eager smile.

"Well, it's not," her cousin said, tartly. "There's a lot of tedious work and poking around in other people's business."

"That is true," Rose said. If Tabitha's comment bothered her it didn't show. "We'd just like to hear about your experience at Gladstone House. We're trying to get a sense of what it's like to stay there."

Gemma took a sip of her tea. "It was a life-changing experience," she said.

"Life changing how?" I asked.

"Well, I saw Emmeline, of course. She doesn't appear to everyone, you know."

Tabitha snorted and picked up her cup.

"Usually I stay here with Tabby when I visit," Gemma continued. "But our cousin Margaret had already claimed her spare room. It seemed like the perfect opportunity to try to meet Emmeline." She reached for a cookie. "Do you believe in ghosts, Sarah?"

I felt certain that if I said no it would be the end of the conversation. "I think there are many, many things out there that we don't understand," I said.

Gemma nodded. "Exactly." Then she looked pointedly across the table at her cousin.

"May I ask where you saw Emmeline?" Rose said.

"Oh, out on the lawn. Sadly, we didn't actually come face-to-face. She was waiting for Captain Phillips, the way she always does."

"So you don't believe he had anything to do with her death?"

This time it was Gemma who gave a snort. "Certainly not. He went to the gallows proclaiming his innocence. And after all, Emmeline wouldn't still be here looking for him if he'd killed her, would she?"

I took a sip of my tea so I wouldn't have to answer.

"You know there are people who question Captain Phillips's innocence?" Rose said. She sat with her hands folded in her lap and a sweet expression on her face.

Gemma nodded. "There are people who question everything."

"And nothing," Tabitha muttered.

"I know I seem like a foolish old woman," Gemma said, "but I don't see the harm in believing in a love that's so strong that it doesn't end when the two lovers aren't here anymore. And I'm not the only one who feels that way. That's why so many people come to Gladstone House. They want to see Emmeline. They want to believe that true love never dies." She smiled and reached for her tea.

Rose asked a few more questions about the food and the service at Gladstone House—Gemma spoke highly of both—and I nodded in the appropriate places. We already had what we had come for.

"Well, that certainly was educational," Rose said as the elevator doors closed. "It seems that Mr. Steele could have put Gladstone House out of business if he'd continued with his investigation."

"So who does that give a motive to?" I asked. "Annie and Emily both have alibis."

"I'm afraid at the moment that's a question I don't have an answer to," she said.

Unfortunately, neither did I.

*   *   *

Mr. P. was waiting in the hallway Wednesday morning. He was wearing a yellow slicker and his pants were tucked into a pair of black rubber boots. And he was smiling. It was raining and windy outside so it wasn't the weather that he looked so pleased about.

"I know that look," I said as I picked up Elvis. There was no way he would walk to the car when it was raining. "You figured something out."

The smile got a little wider. "I found Laurel Prescott," Mr. P. said. "She's in England, in Croydon to be specific, visiting family."

"Do you think she could have killed Mark Steele and then skipped town?" I asked.

He shook his head. "I don't think so. First of all, it seems this was a long-planned vacation. And second, Laurel doesn't seem to have a motive to kill Mr. Steele."

I gave a sigh of frustration. "The problem with this case is that all the people who do have motives also all have alibis."

"Very inconsiderate of them," Mr. P. said with just a hint of a smile. "We have a Zoom call scheduled for later this morning. Maybe Laurel will have some idea of who might have killed her co-host."

It struck me that if you gave Mr. P. a computer and an internet connection there wasn't anything he couldn't find eventually. It was equal parts fascinating and frightening.

Rose came out of her apartment carrying a tote bag in one hand and garment bag in the other. I hurried to take the hanger from her. "Thank you," she said.

"What's this?" I asked. I could think of several possibilities.

She held up a hand as though trying to hold off an objection she expected me to make. "I know you told me I didn't need to starch that tablecloth from the flea market but it looked too limp to me." She looked like a defiant fairy with her soft halo of white hair and her lavender rain jacket, chin out, shoulders squared.

"Why do I bother arguing with you?" I asked.

"I've pondered that very question several times myself," Rose said as she made her way past me. "It seems like a waste of your time."

The rain had let up a little by the time we got to Second Chance. Mac had the coffee made and the kettle was on for tea. My first task was to find several books a collector had emailed us about. All five of them were in a storage bin in the workroom. I took photographs of the copyright pages and emailed them to the collector hoping the books were the ones he wanted.

Mr. P.'s Zoom interview started at ten. We'd only had two customers. Mac inclined his head in the direction of the Angels' office. "Go see what's going on. I think I can handle things here."

"Okay," I said. "Come and get me if you need me."

I stood in the open office doorway, just to listen. I could see most of the computer screen. Laurel Prescott was far more outgoing in person, so to speak, than she was on the show. I knew from the episodes of *Night Moves* I had watched that Laurel was Black and curvy, with short, curly hair. I could see now that she had a great smile and an even better laugh away from the constraints of *Night Moves* or maybe it was being away from Mark Steele. Laurel was warm and funny and I found it hard to see how this woman could have killed anyone.

However, she was telling Rose and Mr. P. that it could be said that she *did* have a motive to kill Mark Steele.

"Why do you say that?" Mr. P. asked.

"Because Mark was trying to push me out of *Night Moves*," she said. "It turns out my Q rating was better than his." She paused and frowned. "You know what a Q rating is, right?"

"It's a mathematical measure of the appeal and familiarity of someone or something," Mr. P. said.

Laurel nodded. "It's the grown-up equivalent of counting who got the most Valentines. Anyway, it turns out people thought he was mean and they liked me better. Mark's response was to use his power to shrink my role in the show."

"Did you kill him?" Rose asked.

Laurel didn't seem offended by being asked. "I would never go that far. Don't get me wrong, Mark was a pain in the ass to work with, but that's not a reason to kill someone. Besides, I was offered a new job and I wasn't renewing my contract with *Night Moves*."

"May I ask what the new job is?" Mr. P. said.

"I'm going to be working on a new program that's a cross between *60 Minutes* and *Entertainment Tonight*. It's going to take more of a hard-news look at the entertainment business."

Mr. P. asked Laurel what she'd been doing in North

Harbor. While she'd told Mark and Delia that she wanted to see Gladstone House for herself, what she'd really been doing was trying to see if there was a story for her new show on what went on behind the scenes at *Night Moves*. In the end she decided there wasn't.

Rose and Mr. P. thanked Laurel for her time and ended the call.

I stepped into the office. "I don't think she did it."

"Neither do I," Rose said.

Mr. P. closed the laptop. "I think we're all in agreement that Laurel Prescott didn't kill anyone."

"So now what?" I said.

"I'm going out to give Mac a hand in the shop," Rose said. She smiled at Mr. P., patted my arm and left.

Mr. P. was already stuffing his laptop in his messenger bag. "I'm going to the historical society. You said Glenn told you that he gave Mr. Steele directions to get there. I'd like to find out what he was looking for. I've worked out a family tree for the Gladstones. Maybe I can fill in some gaps. And I want to know if Captain Phillips has any descendants still alive."

I looked out the window. It seemed to have stopped raining.

"I'm perfectly capable of walking, by the way," the old man said. "I may be sweet, but I'm not made of sugar. I won't melt."

"Okay," I said, "but if we're getting a downpour when you're ready to come back, give me a call. Or Mac."

Mr. P. left and I went upstairs to put on my work

clothes. I still had more work to do on my table. "I'll be outside if you need me," I told Mac and Rose.

To my surprise there was a steady stream of cars coming in and out of the parking lot for the next hour. I didn't hear a peep from Rose or Mac and I managed to finish the sanding and started wiping down the table.

Mr. P. returned about quarter to twelve. "Any success?" I asked.

He patted his bag. "I learned that Mr. Steele had been digging into the Gladstones, tracing back the family."

"I guess that's not really a surprise," I said.

"He also seemed to have spent a lot of time with the newspaper accounts from Captain Phillips's trial. Did you know the captain called Emmeline his North Star?"

I shook my head.

"Emmeline had given him a set of gold cuff links," Mr. P. said. "They were oval shaped, gold with a beaded edge and a star etched on each one, with a tiny diamond in the center. One of those cuff links was found next to Emmeline's body. The prosecutor claimed Phillips had lost it when he killed her. Phillips insisted it had come loose when he tried to revive Emmeline."

I had the feeling I'd seen those cuff links. The image of one lone cuff link came into my mind. I hadn't seen the cuff links. I'd seen a necklace that looked just like them. Maud Fitch's necklace.

Mr. P. was looking expectantly at me. He'd said something I'd missed.

I shook my head. "I'm sorry. What did you say?"

"Just that the coverage at the time was very sensationalized."

I brushed dust off my old paint-spattered shirt. "Is that good or bad?" I asked.

"A little of both, I think," he said. "The papers were certainly pandering to their readers' desire for all the prurient details of the crime, which means we can read about all those details now. But it also makes it abundantly clear how biased that trial was and the newspapers of the time contributed to that bias."

Mr. P. headed inside and I started putting everything away. In my head I could see the tiny oval pendant Maud had been wearing the day of the house tour. There had to be a connection to those cuff links. Could Maud have killed Mark Steele?

"No, that doesn't make sense," I said aloud. A robin in a nearby tree cocked its head and looked at me. It seemed to agree with me.

I needed to talk to Maud. I thought about calling her but this was the kind of conversation I needed to have face-to-face. I finished cleaning up and went back inside to change my clothes. Avery arrived. Rose and Mr. P. were having lunch.

"There's something I need to do," I said to Mac. "Can you hold down the fort for a little while? Charlotte won't be here until later. She has a dentist appointment."

"Sure," he said. "Avery and I were going to see if we could find all the pieces for that chess set you bought from Teresa."

"They're all in a box on the top shelf in the closet under the stairs."

"Not exactly," he said. "The box might have somehow gotten knocked down and the pieces might have somehow gone pretty much everywhere."

"I hate it when that happens," I said, deadpan. Then I smiled. "Once you find the pieces get Avery to do an online search. Charlotte is convinced that chess set is worth more than I paid for it."

"Well, you paid five dollars for it so I think she's right but I'll get Avery to see what she can find." I gave his arm a squeeze and went upstairs.

I decided I'd eat when I got back so I changed, grabbed my jacket and bag and left.

Maud Fitch and her wife owned the Hearthstone Inn. The inn was very popular with tourists since it was within walking distance of the downtown but also offered a gorgeous view of West Penobscot Bay. The inn was a three-story mansard-roofed Victorian with high, narrow windows and beautifully restored exterior details. It had been painted in shades of gray with touches of green, white and bronze on the cornices, moldings and other trim. The front door was a deep forest green.

Maud answered the door. "Hi, Sarah," she said with a smile.

"Hi," I said. "I'm sorry to stop by without calling. Is this a bad time?"

She shook her head. "No. What do you need?"

"I need to talk to you about Mark Steele's death."

Her smile faded. "Okay," she said. "Come in. I was

just finishing lunch." She led us into the dining room. "Would you like a cup of tea?"

"I'm fine. Thank you," I said. I took a seat at the table and as quickly as I sat down I had a lap of calico cat.

"Michelangelo!" Maud exclaimed. "Get down!"

"Mrrr," the cat said as though Maud hadn't spoken.

"He's fine," I said, stroking his fur.

"What he is, is spoiled," Maud said.

I smiled at her. "Isn't that the definition of a cat?"

Michelangelo settled himself on my lap and began to purr. Now that I was here I wasn't sure where to start. I noticed that Maud was wearing the necklace, her fingers touching the oval pendant as though it was some kind of talisman. Maybe it was.

"You wear that necklace a lot," I said.

Maud looked at me for a long moment. "You know," she finally said.

"That you're related to Captain Joseph Phillips, yes."

She frowned. "How did you figure it out?"

"Luck mostly," I said. "The description of the cuff links that Emmeline had bought for him matched the pendant I remembered you wearing. The pieces just fit together."

"This is the lone cuff link that was with his things," Maud said. "The other one was evidence in his trial. Joseph's sister, Catherine, had it made into a necklace and wore it until the day she died." She cleared her throat. "She named her son Charles Joseph after her adored big brother. The necklace was passed down in the family to my mother and then to me. Catherine was my great-great-great-grandmother. Captain Phillips was my family. And I didn't kill Mark Steele."

"I know," I said, "Caroline Vega wouldn't lie to give you an alibi."

"No, she wouldn't but it's more than that. I needed Mark alive."

I stared at her for a moment. "Why?'

"I wanted him to prove that Joseph Phillips was railroaded." Her chin came up and something flashed in her eyes.

"You're the one who told him about Gladstone House and the ghost story," I said slowly.

"Yes. And I . . . I encouraged him keep pushing Annie. I didn't know things would end the way they did." She looked away and I could hear the regret in her voice.

"I know you didn't," I said.

"I tried to befriend Annie, you know. I wanted to know more about Emmeline's death but I really did want to get to know her as a person, too. It didn't work." She sighed. "I can tell you that Mark thought the Gladstones were hiding something."

I'd stopping petting Michelangelo and he nudged my hand with his head. "Did he tell you what he thought it was?"

Maud shook her head. "No. And for all I know maybe there was no secret to find, but Mark definitely thought there was."

"Why does this matter so much?" I asked. "Everything happened such a long time ago."

"This is my family," she said. "Joseph deserves to

have his name cleared. Does justice have a time limit?"

"No," I said. "It doesn't."

"Joseph is dead. Someone has to speak for him. I'm that someone."

Mark Steele was also dead. So who was his someone? I wondered.

Chapter 17

I drove back to Second Chance filled with more questions than I had answers. We were no closer to figuring out who killed Mark Steele than the day the Angels took on the case. I remembered my initial reluctance and wondered if maybe that feeling had been right.

I parked the SUV and walked over to the garage workshop to take another look at my table. I ran my hand over the top. It had taken a lot of work, but it was going to be beautiful once I'd finished painting and varnishing the piece. Maybe I should stick to what I was good at and stop playing Nancy Drew.

Mr. P. was in the Angels' office, head bent over several sheets of paper. I tapped on the door and he looked up and smiled. I explained what I'd learned from Maud. I let out a sigh of frustration. "It doesn't get us any closer to the killer," I said.

"Every piece of information is part of the puzzle.

We just don't have enough pieces to make the whole picture yet," he said.

"I should call Michelle and tell her about Maud," I said, "although maybe she already knows."

Mr. P. glanced at the piece of paper he'd been looking at when I walked in. "I have a few things to share with her as well. Would you like me to give her this information as well?"

I nodded. "Yes. Please." I looked at the paper spread across his desk. "Did you find anything interesting?"

"A couple of things," he said, pushing his glasses up his nose. "I found a set of the original plans for Gladstone House. They're fascinating. And I've been working on the Gladstone family tree," he said. "Would you like to see it?"

"I would," I said. He slid the sheet of paper across the desk. "I've gone back as far as Emmeline and Daniel's parents. Emmeline of course had no offspring. Daniel had three sons as far as I can find, but only one, Matthew, survived to adulthood."

I shook my head. "So much loss in that family."

"Matthew married later in life and had one son, Henry. I'm having a little trouble finding out much about him. As a young man he was a bit of a hellion it seems. Then he was sent off to boarding school and didn't come home until the death of his father when Henry was just eighteen. That seemed to be the making of him. He put his wild days behind him and took a job working at the largest bank in town."

"So Henry was Annie's grandfather?"

Mr. P. handed me a photocopy of an old photo of a

child, maybe a year old, in short pants and a white shirt, held by a man who looked to be in his thirties. Based on the nose they had in common the man had to be his father. "This is Henry and Matthew," he said. "The only photograph I've come across of the younger Mr. Gladstone thus far."

"Annie doesn't look anything like them," I said. "She must take after her mother's side of the family, the way Nick takes after Charlotte."

"You can easily tell those two are mother and son," Mr. P. said. "They have the same eyes, the same smile, the same hairline."

"And they have the same stubborn streak."

He smiled. "Discretion being the better part of valor means I'm not going to comment on that."

It was quiet for the rest of the afternoon. Avery continued her research on the chess set. Mac went out to do some rearranging in the workshop and I updated the shop's inventory lists in between helping customers. Gram called to tell me that Annie Hastings had decided to give everyone with house tour tickets a second chance to see Gladstone House on Sunday afternoon. I wasn't sure how Michelle would feel but when I texted her she said she'd like to go. I decided I had no urge to see the second floor again but I would like to see more of the main level.

Since I'd said I was open to trying the new vegetarian restaurant, Jess had decided there was no time like the present. Avery had promised me that it was more than hummus, tofu and salad and had even given me some suggestions on what to order. To my surprise everything was delicious.

"I'm not sure what to say," Jess said. She mock frowned and pressed a fist to her mouth. "Wait a minute. I think I do." She leaned across the table and stage-whispered, "I told you so."

"You're enjoying this, aren't you?" I asked.

"The food? Yes," she said. "The fact that I pried you out of your metaphorical food rut with a vegetarian crowbar, also yes."

I laughed and Jess went on to list all the other types of food she was going to make me try now that I wasn't so firmly entrenched in my rut. I made faces in all the appropriate places.

We ordered a piece of chocolate cake to share for dessert. It was rich and decadent and one of the best slices of chocolate cake I'd ever enjoyed—and I'd had Charlotte's devil's food cake more than once. Looking across the table at Jess I thought how lucky I was that she'd swiped my ad for a roommate from the music department bulletin board all those years ago.

"Maybe I'll bring Nick here for lunch," Jess said, licking frosting from her fork. "He could do with getting out of his food rut, too."

"You're having lunch with Nick?" I said. *Was* there something going on with the two of them?

She nodded. "On Friday."

"Did you spend Valentine's night with him?" I blurted.

"Yes," she said.

I almost choked on my cake. Jess leaned over and thumped me on the back. "Do I need to do the Heimlich?" she asked.

I shook my head and took a drink of water. "I'm all

right," I said. I leaned back in my chair, coughed again and took a couple of deep breaths. "You and Nick really spent the night together for Valentine's?"

She nodded and speared another bite of cake. "I was throwing up and he was holding my hair. Did Nick tell you?"

I took another drink of water. "No, I was out running the next morning and I saw him leaving your place."

Jess licked a bit of icing from her fork and set it down. "I was out with Elin and a friend of hers. They were drinking and I was the designated driver." Elin was Jess's partner in the store. "I had food poisoning. Pretty sure that tuna I had for lunch was a little past the best-before date." She grimaced.

"Anyway, I started to feel crappy pretty quickly. Elin and Eric weren't okay to drive. Nick happened to stop in for takeout. He got them home and he spent the night looking after me. It was about as unsexy a Valentine's Day as you can get."

She looked at me and a grin started to stretch across her face. "Hang on. Did you think Nick and I . . ." She started to laugh. "You did."

I ducked my head. "I just wondered. That's all."

Jess couldn't stop laughing. "So did you think I took advantage of Nick, Nick took advantage of me or we both were so lonely on Valentine's Day we lost our minds?"

"That could have happened," I said somewhat defensively. "And why are you having lunch on Friday?"

That just made her laugh harder. "First of all, have you met us? I promise there's nothing between Nick and me. I'm buying him lunch because he helped me study for my first aid test." She wiped her eyes with the heel of her hand. "Have you been sitting on this suspicion since Valentine's Day?"

"Yes. I didn't want to butt in just in case it was a one-time thing you both regretted or in case it was the beginning of some kind of romance and I didn't want to wreck it." I swiped a hand over my face. "And hearing that all out loud makes me realize how much I overthought the whole thing."

Jess shook her head and smiled. "I know you love me and Dr. Feelgood, but yeah, you did overthink this big-time. You're my best friend and I wouldn't let Nick or any other guy become a secret between us." She picked up her fork again. "I ruined Nick's fancy ass running shoes," she said.

"That you could have kept from me," I said.

Both Cleveland and Teresa showed up on Thursday morning. I did buy from other pickers from time to time but they had become my regulars. Cleveland had his trailer attached to the back of his old truck and it was filled with chairs.

"You know you're just encouraging this weird thing she has for chairs," Mac said to him.

Cleveland smiled. "As addictions go, this one is pretty tame," he said.

I ended up buying a pie safe, two wooden chairs with interesting turned legs, and a set of four very dirty midcentury modern armchairs with wooden arms and legs and upholstered seats and backs.

Cleveland gave me a deal on the set of four chairs because he wasn't sure they could be saved.

"I found them in a chicken coop," he explained.

"What's with you and chicken coops?" I asked. This wasn't the first time he discovered a find in a chicken coop. It also wasn't the first time I'd ended up buying it.

He shrugged. "You like chairs. I like chicken coops."

From Teresa I bought a wicker tray table with folding metal legs and removable tray, some Corning-Ware casserole dishes that I knew would sell as soon as they were on the floor and two sets of incomplete colored Pyrex mixing bowls. I was hopeful that with the odd bowls we already had we'd be able to make at least two complete sets. I also purchased a large bag of assorted My Little Pony toys. We'd had good luck in the past with kids' toys. A selection of troll dolls had been snapped up in forty-eight hours.

Mr. P. was making his third trip to the historical society's archives. "I have an idea," he said to me. "Cross your fingers."

Like almost all of Mr. P.'s ideas this one panned out. He was back in just over an hour with a satisfied gleam in his eye.

"I was looking for any of Emmeline Gladstone's former suitors," he explained as he hung up his jacket.

"And you found one," I said.

He nodded. "Oliver Hall, who, according to a newspaper story from the day, had gotten into an altercation with Emmeline's brother over comments he had made about her just a week before she died."

Charlotte had just come in the back door. "All the Halls in North Harbor are related," she said. "Thanks to one very prolific predecessor. This has to be one of Stella's ancestors."

Stella Hall was a former client of the Angels. She'd help in any way she could.

"I'll call her," Mr. P. said.

I was opening the bag of My Little Pony toys when Mr. P. came by on his way upstairs for a cup of coffee. Stella needed to talk to her third cousin Howard. He was the keeper of the family history.

There were fourteen of the little vinyl horses in the bag. They needed washing and their hair detangled and we'd have to check to see if any of them were collectibles but I was confident that I could double what I'd spent for them.

A quick search on my phone showed me that the first one I'd taken out of the bag was a rare Cranberry Muffins pony. Several of them had sold online for between fifty and sixty dollars each.

Mr. P. came back and set a mug of coffee on the corner of the workbench. "Thank you," I said.

"You're most welcome," he said. He tapped the pocket of his long-sleeved polo shirt where he kept his phone. "Stella was as good as her word. I'm meeting her at the high school track at three thirty. Her cousin Howard is a teacher and a coach there. She says he'll have the boys' baseball team out running at that time. We can talk to him and see what he knows."

I took a sip of my coffee. "I'd be happy to drive you. It's a bit of a walk."

He smiled. "Thank you, my dear, but Mac already offered and I accepted."

"I'm looking forward to seeing what you find out," I said.

"As I said before, every bit of information is a piece of the puzzle."

"Okay, but next time we're getting a smaller puzzle," I said with a grin.

Mac and Mr. P. left about quarter after three. They were back a bit after four. I had just helped a grandfather pick out a guitar as a gift for his grandson when they walked in. Mac smiled and gave me a thumbs-up.

I handed my customer to Avery and walked over to the guys. "Well?" I said.

"It seems it's common knowledge in at least part of the Hall family that Oliver Hall made up the story about Joseph Phillips already having a family just to discredit him. For the record, Stella didn't know."

"Why would he have done that?" I asked.

"Apparently he was hoping that if Captain Phillips's reputation was besmirched he could resume his courtship of Emmeline."

"Well, that didn't work," I said. "And why has the family been sitting on this information for the last almost two hundred years?"

"Shame, I suspect," Mr. P. said. "I'm not certain Stella's cousin would have confessed the truth to us if his son hadn't overheard the conversation and pushed his father to just admit the truth." He patted my arm. "It's another puzzle piece, my dear."

Rose and Mr. P. had plans and walked off together

at the end of the day. Liz arrived to pick up Avery. Mac was heading off to work on his boat. He offered to drop off Charlotte. I told him I'd call when I got home after the jam.

I was about to leave for The Black Bear when Jess called to say the power was off along the harbor front. "Do you want to come down and wait for a bit to see what happens?" she asked.

"Why not?" I said.

Sam had a small generator and some Coleman lanterns. "The show must go on," he said, putting an arm around my shoulders and giving me a hug. "Are you staying?"

I looked at Jess. "I'm in," she said.

I smiled at Sam. "You'll have an audience of at least two."

Jess elbowed me and pointed at the door. Nick had just walked in.

"Make that three," I said.

Sam smiled back at me. "Back in the day your dad and I played for fewer people than that."

There was no food service other than coffee because the coffee makers could run off the generator. When our server brought our coffee she also brought an order of chips and salsa. "On the house," she said with a smile.

The crowd was a lot smaller than usual, mostly all the die-hard regulars. Right before he took the stage Sam came over to our table, holding a guitar.

Nick shook his head. "No way."

"Just for a couple of songs," Sam said. "All the guys aren't here."

"I've barely played in the last couple of weeks," Nick said.

"Doesn't matter," Sam said. "I know how good you are. And if you're not, so what? Look at this crowd. They won't care. They just want to hear a little music."

"Go," I urged. Jess nodded.

Nick sighed. "Fine. If I suck don't say I didn't warn you."

He didn't suck. He was fantastic. And for a moment I saw the fifteen-year-old guy I'd had a crush on all those years ago. About forty-five minutes in I realized the power was back on. I didn't say a word. I didn't want the mood to be broken. And if anyone else noticed they didn't say anything, either.

When Nick came back to the table I threw my arms around him. "Best jam ever," I said. And I meant it.

Friday morning Charlotte and I were making space for an armoire Mac had cleaned up but decided not to refinish when Liz arrived. She wore a camel coat over a black skirt and black boots with heels that looked like lethal weapons. "Are Rose and Alfred here?" she asked.

I shook my head. "They'll be here later. They had some kind of meeting at the library."

"That's fine," she said. "You'll do. I asked Channing to see what he could find out about the Hastingses' financial situation. I thought it might be useful information to have."

"What did you find out?" I asked.

"Things are more precarious than Annie has been letting on. Channing discovered that house has been mortgaged multiple times over the years. The bookings for the bed-and-breakfast are barely keeping things afloat and one of the main attractions seems to be that ridiculous ghost story."

"It sounds like things were a very precarious house of cards," Charlotte said.

"So if Mark Steele had managed to make it seem as though the ghost of Emmeline wasn't real, Annie and Emily might have lost the house," I said slowly. I felt some of the puzzle pieces snap together. What did Nick always say? *Who benefits?*

"It seems to me the Hastingses had the most to gain from Mr. Steele's death," Liz said. "Is it possible that Emily Hastings faked her alibi?"

Chapter 18

Liz left for her office a few minutes later.

"Do you think she's right?" I said to Charlotte. "Do you think Emily faked the car breaking down?"

"I don't want to believe it," Charlotte said. "And would it even be possible?"

I raked a hand through my hair. "I don't know. I'm not even sure what the problem was. Maybe a flat tire?"

"What do you know?" she said.

"Maud and Caroline were at Gladstone House helping with a few last-minute details. Annie accidentally knocked over a cup of tea and it stained the tablecloth. She's particular about the small details and didn't want to put a cloth on the table that was too modern."

"That makes sense," Charlotte said. "I'd be the same way."

"Emily went to borrow a cloth from someone they knew. It's a big table. An average tablecloth wouldn't fit. The car broke down. Emily had to wait for a tow truck and she wasn't back by the time the tour started."

Charlotte frowned. "Whose car was it?"

"Emily's," I said.

She shook her head. "I don't think so. To the best of my knowledge Emily doesn't have a car. She rides her bike everywhere."

She was right. I'd seen Emily all over town on her bike, in good weather and bad. "I don't know then. Maybe the car is Annie's."

"She must have had a receipt from the tow truck driver and Michelle would have checked that."

I leaned down and straightened a quilt that was draped over the back of an old metal trunk. "Do you think something like that could be faked?"

Charlotte smiled. "I've seen students fake pretty much everything from exams to essays to notes from doctors claiming they have gout and can't take gym class so I'm pretty sure a receipt from a towing company could be faked but wouldn't the police have checked with the company?"

"Yeah, they would have," I said, straightening up. "What if the tow truck driver helped Emily fake her alibi? What if she used her womanly wiles on him?"

Charlotte laughed. "Womanly wiles? Are you protecting my delicate sensibilities or your own?"

I felt my cheeks redden. "I was trying to be polite."

"Using her so-called womanly wiles would be a risky idea. The more people who know a secret the less likely it is to be a secret very long. And Emily doesn't strike me as the femme fatale type." She adjusted the front of her apron. "Talk to Alfred or Rose and see what they think. I don't think I can help you with this. But I'm hoping I can help in some other way."

"Do you have something specific in mind?"

"Clayton gave me a couple of boxes of old books and papers that belonged to his grandmother. I started going through it all last night and Avery is going to help me tonight."

"What are you looking for?"

Charlotte shook her head. "I don't know but Clayton said there are a couple of journals and a collection of essays about life in North Harbor in the mid-1800s in there. Maybe I'll find something to help."

I kissed her cheek and headed up to my office to put on my painting clothes.

I painted the legs and the drawer of my farm table and discovered that six of the ponies were considered collectibles. I set Avery to work photographing all fourteen and listing them on the website.

Mac came out to the workshop as I was putting away my painting gear. "How about I cook supper?" he said.

I was dusty and tired and the suggestion was the best one I'd heard all day. "Yes," I said.

"Don't you want to know what I'm making?" he asked.

I shook my head. "I don't. I don't care if you give me a grilled-cheese sandwich or a five-course meal. I will happily eat whatever you cook for me."

What he did cook for me was fish tacos—crispy fish coated with cayenne and cumin, corn tortillas, broccoli slaw and a sprinkle of shredded cheddar. "I think my happy place is anywhere you're cooking for me," I said. Elvis meowed his agreement from the floor, where he was eating a small piece of plain fish Mac had cooked for him.

Mac smiled. "Mine too," he said.

Saturday morning I got up early and went for a long run. While my feet hit the pavement I tried to come up with a way to figure out if Emily Hastings had killed Mark Steele. I knew that Gladstone House meant everything to Annie and I wondered how far Emily would go for her grandmother.

Avery and Charlotte were waiting for me by the back door. I knew something was up because Avery was literally bouncing up and down on the balls of her feet.

"You two are early," I said. "What's going on?"

"You tell her because you found it," Charlotte said.

"We found a diary of a woman who got bodies ready to get buried," Avery said. "She kept these really detailed notes and one of the people was Emmeline Gladstone. There's all this stuff about the body. I want to show what I found—what we found"—she looked at Charlotte—"to Mr. P. Maybe he can use it to figure out who killed Emmeline."

"I think that's a great idea," I said.

When the old man arrived about five minutes after we opened I sent Avery off to the Angels' office to show him what she found.

"That child is so smart," Charlotte said. "I would have missed the information about the body altogether. At best I would have flipped through the journal and just set it aside."

"It was good of Clayton to give you those boxes from his grandmother," I said. "We really need to thank him." I looked at Charlotte and raised an eyebrow. "I'm sure you'll think of something. Rose's flourless chocolate cake is good." I continued to eye Charlotte without speaking until she blushed.

"Fine. I've been seeing Clayton," she said.

I grinned at her as I clapped—quietly—and jumped up and down.

"But I want to keep that between us for now. Or maybe forever."

I stopped jumping. "Why?"

"Nick. Maddie tried to set me up with a friend of hers and you'd think she'd suggested I dance in my underwear on the boardwalk."

I put one arm around her shoulders. "Do that and I promise you'll be beating off the men with a stick."

She gave me the side-eye and shook her head. "I think as far as Nicolas is concerned I'm supposed to be a nun for the rest of my life."

"Your personal life is none of my business," I said, "but since you and your merry band of meddlers have had their fingers in *my* personal life pretty much for as long as I can remember I'm going to say one thing. I love Nick like he was another brother and you should tell him to blow it out his ear."

Charlotte laughed. A customer came in then, looking for a set of nice dishes for an upcoming family dinner, which put an end to our conversation.

"I want something pretty because our everyday dishes are a mismatched set," the woman said. "I have four boys. But I don't want something expensive, because *I have four boys.*"

"I would suggest a set of all-white dishes," Charlotte said. She looked at me and I nodded in agreement. "They're easy to coordinate with other pieces and when you—or someone—breaks a dish it's not difficult to find a replacement. And if you set the table with a flowered or a patterned tablecloth the whole thing will look pretty but the spills won't show as easily."

"Do you have any of those tablecloths?" she asked.

"I can think of a couple that might work for you," I said.

We ended up selling her a set of all-white dishes for a very reasonable price along with a bold flowered tablecloth that would hide just about anything those four boys could spill on it.

I realized there was no coffee or tea made yet because neither Rose nor Mac had arrived. The latter had seen an ad online for a chrome dining set at a yard sale and had set off early to take a look. I wasn't sure where Rose was. She wasn't due until after lunch.

"I'm going to put the kettle on," I said to Charlotte.

"What a splendid idea," she said.

I looked around. "Do you know where Elvis is?" Usually he would have been up on a chair, sharing his opinion on tablecloths with our customer.

"I think he's in with Avery and Alfred," Charlotte said.

I made the coffee and a pot of tea. I poured a cup of

coffee for myself and a cup of tea for Charlotte, who was now going through our tablecloth collection. Then I went out to the Angels' office.

Mr. P. and Avery were at the big table, their heads bent over an old leather-bound book. I knocked on the doorframe and they both looked up. "I made tea and coffee," I said.

"Perfect timing," Mr. P. said. "I was just thinking I'd like a cup."

"Charlotte brought apple-spice muffins," I said to Avery. "Want one?"

She nodded.

I turned to go get everything and Mr. P. said, "I think we might have found something. This diary that Avery discovered is proving to be very enlightening."

I stopped in my tracks and turned around. "Can I see?"

He nodded and beckoned me over.

The writing in the journal was all in meticulous cursive and there were some small drawings interspersed between the written words.

"This woman seemed to have some medical knowledge," Mr. P. explained. "She noticed things the doctor who examined the body and who testified at the trial didn't see."

"Such as?"

He nudged his glasses up his nose. "Well, she made note of some petechial hemorrhaging and some swelling around the throat. The doctor did talk about both of those at the trial. But Clara—that's her name, Clara McKinnon—also saw some rash on Emmeline's chest and she spotted what she believed to be an insect sting just below her left ear.

"The hemorrhaging in her eyes and the swelling in her throat are consistent with strangling but the other details Clara noted, the rash and the insect sting, taken together with the first two suggest that Emmeline Gladstone died from an allergic reaction." He and Avery smiled at each other.

I stared at them. "She wasn't murdered," I said slowly.

"I don't think so," Mr. P. said. "Someone who has more medical expertise should look at these notes but based on what I've seen here, Captain Phillips didn't murder that young woman and neither did anyone else."

"He was innocent."

Mr. P. nodded. "Yes."

I looked at Avery. "No one would know this without you."

"I just read some stuff in an old book," she said.

I gestured at the journal. "You're the first person in close to two hundred years who paid attention to what was written in that old book. You did good. You did really good."

She smiled and ducked her head.

"At some point we need to tell Maud Fitch," I said to Mr. P.

"I agree," he said. "But for now I think we need to keep this particular piece of information to ourselves until we figure out if it fits and where."

"I agree," I said.

We both looked at Avery.

"I don't think anyone I know would care," she said, "but I won't say anything."

I looked around the office. "Was Elvis with you?"

"I haven't seen him this morning," Mr. P. said.

"The furball is probably sleeping on your desk," Avery said. "I'm going to get a muffin." She looked at Mr. P. "And I'll get your coffee."

He smiled at her. "Thank you."

Elvis wasn't on the workbench or anywhere in the workroom. He wasn't in the shop, either, and Avery said she couldn't find him anywhere upstairs.

"I'm going out to make sure he didn't wander over to the workshop," I said. Elvis wasn't there. He wasn't hiding under my car, either. How could a small black cat seemingly vanish?

I was about to text Mac to see if he had any ideas when I saw Emily Hastings coming along the sidewalk with Elvis in the wicker basket of her bike.

I felt a rush of relief.

Emily raised a hand in hello when she spotted me. I walked down to meet them.

"Hi, Sarah," she said. "I found this guy two streets over just sitting at the corner. I thought I better bring him back." She reached down to stroke his fur.

"Thank you," I said. "We've been looking everywhere for him. He's never wandered off like that before." I looked at Elvis. "What were you doing?"

He ignored me and nuzzled Emily's hand.

"I think you have a friend for life," I said.

She smiled. "Elvis is a great cat. I'd like to have a

cat of my own but some guests can be allergic or just afraid of them." She looked down at Elvis. "How could anyone be afraid of him?"

Elvis murped his agreement.

"How's the case going?" Emily asked.

"Mr. P. is working on a couple of things," I said.

Looking at Emily standing there scratching behind Elvis's ear I just couldn't believe she had killed Mark Steele. With her warm smile and kind eyes I couldn't imagine her stomping on a cockroach.

"Good," she said. "I wish I knew who killed Mr. Steele or that there was at least some kind of way I could help figure that out. And I really wish that stupid car of Gram's hadn't gotten a flat tire."

So she had been driving Annie's car. "I know," I said.

"Gram says I'm lucky. Because of that flat tire everyone knows I didn't kill Mr. Steele, but if that hadn't happened, I might have been a suspect." She shook her head. "I better get going," she said. She picked Elvis up and handed him to me.

"Thanks again for rescuing him," I said. "You're welcome to stop in and visit him any time. He really does like you."

"Thanks," she said. "I will." Emily waved to Elvis, got on her bike and rode away.

I shifted the cat so we were face-to-face. "You scared me," I said.

He licked my chin.

I thought about the expression on his face while Emily was stroking his fur and talking about the murder. He had looked blissfully happy the entire time. No sour look of annoyance.

"Did you go looking for Emily?" I asked.

He didn't blink or so much as twitch a whisker. I realized how crazy what I was thinking was. My cat hadn't orchestrated a meeting between Emily and me so he could prove she hadn't killed Mark Steele. That wasn't possible. He'd just gotten bored and wandered off while Charlotte and I were talking. It was the only thing that made sense. That and the fact that Emily Hastings wasn't our killer.

So now what?

Chapter 19

I went back inside and told everyone how I'd found Elvis. "Dude, what were you thinking?" Avery said.

He almost seemed to shrug.

"There are some orders to be packed on the workbench," I said to Avery, "and then could you do half a dozen more teacup planters, please?"

"Sure," she said. "Want me to take the King of Rock and Roll and keep an eye on him?"

"Yes, please," I said. I handed over Elvis, who seemed quite happy to go with Avery.

Once they were gone I told Mr. P. and Charlotte about my conversation with Emily.

Mr. P. took off his glasses and cleaned them with the little cloth he always carried in his pocket. "I know it seems somewhat unorthodox, but Elvis has never been wrong about this kind of thing."

"Well, I'm happy," Charlotte said. "I didn't like the idea that Emily had killed Mr. Steele."

"Neither did I," I said.

"So we keep going," Mr. P. said. He explained that he had copies of a bunch of the documents and photos that he believed Mark Steele had looked at while he was at the historical society. "I'm going to look through them to see if anything seems significant."

I decided I'd spend some time working on my table. I went upstairs to change and grabbed a cup of coffee to take outside with me. It was dull and cool but there wasn't any rain in the forecast. "Fire off a flare if you need me," I told Charlotte.

I'd just gotten my tarp down when Mac pulled in. The table and chairs were in the back of his truck. There were four mint green chairs and a lighter green Formica table.

"Nice," I said, walking around the bed of the truck so I could see the table from both sides.

"It's sticky and dirty and ridiculously underpriced," Mac said.

I turned to look at him. "I sense a story."

He reached into the truck and took a large cardboard box off the front seat. "Not much of one. The guy who sold all of this to me was happy to get rid of what he called old-people furniture."

I groaned. "I hate it when people don't recognize quality." I dropped the tailgate of the truck and climbed up into the back so I could look at the table and chairs up close. I checked the chairs from end to end and went all over the Formica table as well, even getting down on my knees to look at the underside.

"Well?" Mac said.

I backed out from under the table and sat back on my heels. "I'm pretty sure it's 1950s vintage. I can't get over what incredible shape it's in after all these years. It doesn't look like it's been used in a long time."

"I don't think it has," he said. "From what I saw it's been sitting in this guy's basement since it came from his grandmother's house."

I stood up, brushing some dried leaves from last fall off my jeans.

Mac handed me a piece of paper.

"What's this?" I said.

He smiled. "I knew you'd want to see what else he has. We can go take a look Monday night. That's his cell number and the address. His name is Jeremy."

I jumped down from the back of the truck and flung my arms around him. "There will be a little something extra with your stipend this week," I said, waggling my eyebrows at him.

As we unloaded the table and chairs I brought Mac up-to-date on the morning so far and Elvis's adventures. "I'm with Alfred," he said. "It's not like you have any tangible evidence to link Emily to Mark Steele's murder and Elvis has never steered you wrong before. I don't know how he does it but he's reading something in people. He's a feline polygraph with a better reliability rate than a machine."

I gestured at the box that Mac had taken out of the front seat of the truck. "What else did you buy?" I asked.

"A bunch of old LPs. I thought we could display the albums and the two remaining record players together and maybe they'd be more likely to sell."

Once we had everything stashed in the workshop and covered with a tarp Mac went in to get coffee.

"I'm going to grab Avery if that's okay and make sure the albums are playable and that none of them are more valuable than I think."

"Go ahead," I said. "She was packing some parcels but she's probably done by now."

I had just finished the second coat of paint on the table when I saw Mr. P. coming across the parking lot. "Sarah, may I borrow your eyes for a minute?"

"Sure," I said.

He was holding several sheets of paper. He set one down on top of a tea cart that I'd forgotten to ask Mac to take into the shop. "This is a very nice piece," Mr. P. said.

"It's walnut, for the most part," I said. "I'm not sure how old it is but I'm confident it's pre-1880 because of the square screws." I smiled. "You have excellent taste, which I already knew because you chose Rose."

He smiled back at me. "I think it was Rosie who chose me but I'll take the compliment." He tapped the paper he'd laid down. It was a copy of a photograph. His expression turned serious. "What do you see?" he said.

"That's Annie and Emily." The photo looked like it had been taken in the parlor at Gladstone House.

Mr. P. hiked his pants up a little. "They're related."

I nodded. "You know they are. They're grand-mother and granddaughter."

It seemed to be what he'd wanted to hear me say. He smiled again. "How do you know?"

I had no idea what he was getting at. I rubbed a hand over the back of my neck. "I don't know. They're part of the same family. They have the same last name. They look alike."

"So they have a biological connection?"

"Yes." I didn't know what he was getting at but we seemed to be taking the long way around the farm. I picked up the photocopy. "Look. Both Annie and Emily tip their heads to the left in the same way. They have the same jawline and the same nose." I traced my finger down Annie's nose and then Emily's.

"It's a Greek nose," Mr. P. said. "Very straight and symmetrical. It's only seen in a small amount of the population."

He set down another copy of a photo. This one was of an older man. "Do you know who this is?"

The man looked to be in his late sixties. "No," I said. "But he had to be related to Annie and Emily. He has the same jawline and the same nose. And look." I tapped the image. "He's even tilting his head a little to the left."

"Very observant," Mr. P. said.

I folded my arms across my chest and tried to guess the age of the picture. "Is that Annie's father?"

He nodded. "Yes, it's Jacob Gladstone."

He handed me another picture. This was beginning to feel like the children's memory game where you had to find the matching pairs.

This man looked very much like Jacob Gladstone. He appeared to be somewhere in his late seventies or early eighties. He had a full head of thick white hair and a serious expression on his face. A scar cut across his chin. Another ran from the outer edge of his left eyebrow down his cheek to the corner of his nose. He seemed to have the same traits that Jacob shared with Annie and Emily: the straight nose, the strong jaw. As well, the two men had the same straight, thick hair.

"That's Jacob's father, isn't it?" I said.

"Yes," Mr. P. said. "That is Henry Gladstone. You can't tell from the photographs, because they're black-and-white, but I found several references to both men having hazel eyes."

"Annie has hazel eyes," I said. "And Emily does, too."

Mr. P. took off his glasses, rubbed the bridge of his nose and put them on again. "There are very few photos of Henry Gladstone as an adult, I've learned. It appears that he was averse to getting his photo taken."

"You showed me a photo of Henry when he was a baby."

He nodded and put yet another copy of a photograph on the tea cart. This one was a photo of a young man of about seventeen or so. "Mark Steele looked at this photo several times. Eli, the young man working at the archives, told me that Mr. Steele tried to take it over to the window to get a better look at it and he had to stop him. The next day Mr. Steele came back with a lighted magnifier."

I looked at the picture again. "Do you have any idea why he was so interested in this particular photo?"

He nodded. "I think I do, but I want to see what you think without biasing you."

I picked up the piece of paper. "Okay. I think this person could be related to the Phillips family."

"Why do you say that?" Mr. P. said.

"You've shown me all these photos of the Glad-stones." I gestured at the table. "And this man doesn't look like any of them. Look at his nose." I pointed. "It's completely different from what you called the Greek nose that all the Gladstones you showed me have. This man's nose is larger and more prominent."

He dipped his head. "You would be correct," he said.

"This man's jawline is thicker and he has a bit of wave to his hair. Even though it's all slicked down I can see a bit of curl on one side. Since the Gladstones and the Phillipses are the two families tied up in all of this I think this man, whoever he is, is a member of the Phillips family."

"This is Henry Gladstone at seventeen."

I shook my head. "That's not possible." I picked up the two images of young Henry and old Henry and studied them side by side. After a moment I shook my head and held out the photograph of the younger man. "This one has been mislabeled or misidentified at the historical society. These are not photos of the same man. Their facial structure is too different."

"I had the same thought," Mr. P. said. "But the photo of the younger man is definitely Henry Glad-stone. I found another photo of him. There's no doubt. It's Henry."

I folded my arm up over the top of my head. "It doesn't make sense."

"It does if the older man isn't Henry."

If the older man isn't Henry, he'd said.

I frowned. "So you think someone was masquerading as Henry Gladstone?"

Mr. P. nodded. "Essentially, yes." He handed me the final piece of paper he was holding. It was a copy of a newspaper article about a train derailment. "Henry Gladstone was in school in Boston. He was called home when his father died. He hadn't been back to North Harbor in years."

"He was on that train."

"Yes. You saw the scars on the older Henry's face. They came from that accident. He spent ten days in hospital. At first he had some memory-loss issues and he walked with a limp for quite a while, but he was no longer the reckless young man he'd been. I think that's because he literally *was* no longer that man."

"I don't understand," I said. "What happened?"

He smoothed one hand back over his head. "This is just speculation on my part," he said. "But I believe I'm right. Another young man from Henry's school was on that train—Peter Alexander. They were friends it seems. Peter died in the accident along with three other people. What I think really happened is that Peter, who was orphaned and only had a great uncle left as family, took on Henry's life. Possibly he was even mistaken for Henry at first. No one had seen Henry Gladstone for years. He'd left a boy and come home a young man. And the accident was the perfect way to cover up all the things he didn't know and the people he didn't recognize."

"I don't know," I said. "How would he have been able to pull that off?"

"It was a long time ago. Over a hundred years. No

internet. No social media. Not even a lot of photographs being taken. People here were expecting to see Henry Gladstone and that's what they saw. Everything else could be explained by the accident. And keep in mind, Henry and Peter Alexander knew each other so the latter likely knew at least a little about Henry's life. I think Mr. Alexander saw an opportunity for a better life than what he was facing and he took it. He just slid seamlessly into Henry's life."

"Do you think Annie or Emily know?"

"I couldn't even begin to guess," he said.

"You think Mark Steele came to the same conclusion as you have, though."

"I do. Revealing this subterfuge would be a way to have increased the viewership of his show in his mind."

"So all of this was just about ratings."

"Sadly, I think so. I think we need to talk to Annie."

"Do you want to wait for Rose?" I asked.

He adjusted his glasses again. "Normally I would say yes, but Rosie will be tied up at the library until late this afternoon, and when I was talking to Eli at the historical society, he let it slip that Delia Watson has been in twice in the last couple of days."

I blew out a breath. "You think she's trying to learn what Mr. Steele was digging into."

"I'm afraid so. And remember, they're opening up Gladstone House to people who had tour tickets tomorrow. That includes Delia."

"Give me fifteen minutes," I said. "I just need to wash my brushes and change my clothes and we can go talk to Annie."

"Thank you, my dear," Mr. P. said. "I think this is a conversation better had in person than over the phone."

I picked up the little bucket of water holding my brushes. This case had a lot more similarity to a maze than it did a puzzle, I realized. We were getting in deeper and deeper and there didn't seem to be a clear way out.

Chapter 20

Mr. P. and I drove over to Gladstone House. I felt . . . unsettled, as though something was staring me in the face and for some reason I just couldn't see it. Was I wrong about Emily? Was I crazy to basically decide she wasn't a killer because of something Elvis hadn't done?

When we got to Gladstone House I turned my phone off. We didn't need any distractions while we were talking. Annie was home. Emily wasn't. "She's gone to the store to get some things she needs to make cookies for tomorrow," Annie said.

Mr. P. explained that there was something we needed to talk to her about and she invited us in.

Once again the house was immaculate, hardwood floors gleaming and every surface polished and dust free. There was a beautiful old lace tablecloth on the long dining room table. Annie followed my gaze. "I was able to get the tea stain out," she said.

"The table looks beautiful with that cloth and the candleholders," I said. "The entire house is beautiful."

"Thank you," Annie said.

I noticed that there were two lush arrangements of pale pink roses, one on the table and one I could see in the parlor.

Annie smiled. "I learned my lesson," she said. "This time we were very careful not to let the flowers get cold. I even picked them up a day early so if there was a problem there would be time to get more. Last time was the perfect storm of things going wrong and that won't happen again."

Mr. P. was studying an old photograph that looked like it had been taken along the harbor front. Annie made her way over to him.

I glanced around. Annie was right. What occurred the day of Mark Steele's murder *was* the perfect mix of things happening. Too perfect, if that could be said about a chain of events that ended with someone dead. If one thing had been different Mark Steele would be alive. How did that old proverb go? For want of a nail? I had a sudden gnawing feeling in my stomach.

Mr. P. and Annie were discussing the history of the house. "Emily is the eighth generation to live here," I heard her say.

He gestured at the fireplace. "Those are Damariscotta River bricks, aren't they?"

She nodded. "They were made before I was born, and they'll be here long after I'm gone."

"I love old houses," Mr. P. said. "They all have a story."

"Yes they do," Annie said. "Some of it good. Some of it not so good."

"Do you think that speculation that the house was designed by Irish architect Henry Rowe could be true?" he asked.

Annie leaned heavily on her cane. "I'd like to believe it is. Most experts insist his earliest commission in Maine was the Gothic House in Portland, but family lore says it was actually Gladstone House. Just another chapter to the story, I guess. Come into the parlor. It's a more comfortable space to talk."

We moved across the hall. The parlor was a beautiful space with a wall of bookshelves at the far end and lots of light coming through the windows that faced the street.

Annie smiled. "I was about to have a cup of tea. Would either of you like one?"

Mr. P. said no and so did I.

"Could I help you?" I asked.

"Thank you," Annie said, "but I can manage. I'm going to be a heathen and have my tea in a mug, which is easier to carry, and the doctor says I need to keep moving or I'll end up not being able to move at all. I'll be right back."

Mr. P. was looking at another old photograph. I walked over to the bookshelves. Most of the volumes were classics. The Brontë sisters. Dickens. Louisa May Alcott. Sir Arthur Conan Doyle. A copy of *The Return of Sherlock Holmes* was lying on a small table to the right of the bookshelves. I stood there, unmoving, staring at the collection of short stories. To continue with Alfred's metaphor the puzzle pieces began to snap into place.

My mind was churning and I could taste something sour in the back of my throat. I swung around. "I, umm, I think I should go help Annie," I said. I headed for the kitchen before he could say anything.

When got there I stood back in the hall and watched Annie, trying to stay out of her sight line and not make a sound. She moved carefully around the room with her cane. I took note of the way she was deliberate about every movement. Was I wrong? Had I just made a giant mental leap and fallen flat on my face?

Annie took the lid off the china sugar bowl sitting on the kitchen counter. She pulled a metal canister closer, took off the top, looked inside and then gave a sigh of frustration. For a moment she just stood there. Then she seemed to make up her mind. She hooked the end of her cane on one of the drawer pulls, stood up on her tiptoes and lifted a bag of sugar from the shelf of one of the kitchen cupboards. She set it on the counter and I watched as she opened the bag, filled the canister and then the empty sugar bowl. She didn't struggle, she didn't grimace, she didn't even wince in pain. She moved as effortlessly as I did in my own kitchen.

Annie Hastings was not disabled.

Which meant Annie Hastings had killed Mark Steele. I slowly backed up and hurried to the living room. Mr. P. turned to look at me. I grabbed his arm. "We have to get out of here. Right now." I pulled my phone out of my pocket and realized I'd turned it off. Why had I done that? Why hadn't I put it on silent instead?

"Where's Annie? What are you talking about?" Mr. P. said.

From behind us Annie said, "She figured it out."

I turned to face her, stepping in front of Mr. P. She didn't have her cane. She did have a gun.

"Yes, I did," I said, surprised that my voice wasn't shaking. The rest of me seemed to be.

"You killed Mark Steele," Mr. P. said.

Annie nodded. "I did."

"You don't have arthritis," I said.

"No, I don't." She held up her right hand. "Well, except for a bit of wear and tear in this little finger."

"I wasn't quiet enough," I said. I didn't think I'd given myself away when I was watching her in the kitchen.

She gave an offhand shrug. "To be fair, I have excellent hearing. Out of curiosity, how did you figure it out?"

"Who benefits," I said. "I kept asking myself that question and it was always you but you had an alibi. Then I was looking at your bookshelves and I noticed a copy of *The Return of Sherlock Holmes*, there on that table." I pointed behind her.

"Emily is reading it." She didn't turn to look and my fantasy that I could push Mr. P. away and get the jump on her faded.

"The book contains the short story 'The Adventure of the Empty House.'" Out of the corner of my eye I saw Mr. P. nod. He had gotten the reference. Annie was frowning. She hadn't.

"This is how the reader learns that Sherlock Holmes faked his death. He didn't really die in Switzerland falling into a gorge with his archenemy Moriarty. It suddenly hit me that you could have faked your immobility. It was the perfect way to make it seem like the ghost of Emmeline was haunting the house. You could sneak around and no one would ever suspect you."

Annie nodded. "Your grandmother said you were a smart cookie."

"You knew about your grandfather," Mr. P. said. He took a step forward so we were standing side by side.

"Knew what?" she said. I saw the corner of her right eye twitch.

"That your grandfather was actually a man named Peter Alexander."

For a long moment she looked at us without saying a word. The she sighed softly. "Yes, I knew. My grandfather suffered from dementia. He told me before he died."

"You didn't tell anyone," I said. Maybe I could keep her talking until Emily came back.

"Of course I didn't." I saw a flash of anger in her eyes. "Gladstone House and the Gladstone lineage are all I have to leave Emily. I did a little research into Peter Alexander's family tree. They were nothing but con artists and reprobates with nothing but debts to their name. My grandfather wanted better for himself and I want better for my granddaughter. Mark Steele was going to take it all away."

"He saw the photos of Henry, young and old," Mr. P. said.

"He was going to tell your secret. All of your secrets," I said.

Annie looked away for a brief moment. "This was none of his business. When I said no he should have accepted that."

"You called and asked him to meet you before the tour, while Maud and Caroline were gone."

"Yes, I did." Her chin came up. "I thought maybe I could reason with him."

"You stained the tablecloth on purpose and you did something to Emily's tire so she wouldn't be a suspect."

"You make it sound like I planned to kill Mark," she said. "I didn't. I just . . . I just lashed out in anger."

I wasn't so sure about that. I couldn't see any remorse in Annie right now and I was very aware that she used to be a nurse and would know exactly where to stab Mr. Steele.

"Please put the gun down," I said. "You can't shoot us. Emily will be back any minute now."

Before she could answer the doorbell rang. Annie's face hardened. "Not a sound," she said in a harsh voice. Her eyes met mine. "I will kill him." I realized the gun was aimed directly at Mr. P.

The doorbell rang again. Annie stepped over to the bookcases at the end of the room and grabbed the inside edge of the third shelf in the first bookcase. The whole thing swung open. There was some kind of hidden passage back there. My heart began to hammer in my chest.

"So that's where it is," Mr. P. said. "Fascinating." He looked at me. "I told you I saw the original plans for the house."

"Go," Annie said, gesturing with the gun.

Inside the space there was a narrow set of stairs. We started up them. I was conscious of Annie behind us. I felt a burn of panic in my chest and I forced it down. There had to be a way out of this. If I could push Alfred to one side when we got to the top of these stairs I could rush Annie and get the gun. A little laugh of hysterical laughter came out. "Annie get your gun," I mumbled.

"What did you say?" Mr. P. whispered.

"Be quiet," Annie ordered.

We continued up the stairs and came out, via a closet, into the room where she had killed Mark Steele. Annie jammed the gun in my back and I had no chance to get Mr. P. out of the way.

"We're going down the hall to the little door at the end," she said. "And then we're going up to the attic from there."

"Are you going to push us off the roof?" Mr. P. asked.

"You and Sarah will be up there looking for clues on the widow's walk," Annie said. "I couldn't follow you, of course. You will lose your footing and fall and Sarah will die trying to save you. Tragic really."

"A fall from that height might not kill us," I said.

"I've done the math. I'm confident it will."

"The median lethal distance for falling is approximately forty-eight feet," Mr. P. said.

I should have known he'd know that.

"I would estimate the height of the ceilings on this floor and the one below us to be nine feet. Allowing about nine more feet for the attic means the total distance we would fall would be twenty-seven feet." He looked at me. "The odds are in our favor."

I nodded. "Good to know."

Annie waved the gun in the direction of the hall. "Let's go," she said.

Behind her I thought I saw a flash of movement. Had I imagined it?

I shook my head. "No. If you want us dead you can shoot us," I said with more bravado in my voice than I felt.

I saw a flicker of a shadow move on the hall floor behind her. Someone *was* out there.

"I could shoot you," Annie said, "and just leave your bodies to decompose in the passageway."

"It's not airtight," I said. "Someone will notice."

"I'm not having this conversation with you," she said. "Move."

I squared my shoulders. "No."

The huge vase of roses that had been on the dining room table appeared in the doorway behind Annie. I hoped Mr. P. saw it, too.

"This is your last chance." Annie raised the gun and the vase smashed over the back of her head. She crumpled to the ground. Rose rushed across the room and wrapped her arms around Mr. P. She reached out one hand to touch my cheek. "Are you both all right?" she said.

"We're fine," Mr. P. said.

I nodded. "We need to call the police."

"Oh, I already did that," Rose said. And right on cue I heard the wail of sirens in the background. It was over.

Chapter 21

I bent down to make sure that Annie was breathing. She was. The gun had skidded across the hardwood floor and under the bed against the end wall. I left it there.

Rose and Mr. P. went downstairs to let the police in. I sat down on the edge of the bed. I was still shaking.

I heard Michelle call my name. I got to my feet again and made my way around Annie, over to the door. She was beginning to regain consciousness. I heard her moan softly.

Michelle was partway up the stairs, her face tight with concern. Two paramedics were right behind her.

"Right here," I said, holding up one hand.

Her shoulders sagged with relief. "You all right?" she asked.

I nodded.

"Where's Annie?"

I pointed over my shoulder.

Michelle came down the hall, looked into the

bedroom and gestured to the paramedics. Annie was starting to move. Michelle and I stepped back out of their way. "What happened?" she asked.

I exhaled slowly. "Mr. P. and I came to talk to Annie. He'd found some information about her family that we thought she should know. I saw her in the kitchen and realized she's faking her inability to get around."

She frowned. "Are you certain?"

I didn't blame her for doubting me. "Very," I said. "Talk to Rose and Mr. P. and if you need more proof her gun is under the bed." I gestured over my shoulder.

"She held the three of you at gunpoint."

"She held Mr. P. and me at gunpoint. Rose rescued us."

For a moment Michelle just looked at me, incredulous. "Rose Jackson took on a woman with a gun."

I nodded. "She did. With a large vase of flowers."

"Okay," she said slowly. "I have a feeling there's a lot more to this story but that will do for now. Would you go wait for me downstairs, please?"

"Sure," I said. I was finding the smell of the roses cloying.

Michelle put a hand on my arm. "I'm glad you're all right."

I put my hand over hers for a moment and gave it a squeeze. Then I went downstairs.

Rose and Mr. P. were in the dining room. "You're both okay?" I said.

"We're fine, my dear," Mr. P. said. "Are you sure you're not hurt?"

"I'm sure," I said. I looked at Rose. "How did you

figure this all out? And how did you know we were in trouble?"

"I called Alfred," she said. "I'd found out that Mr. Steele had been in the library trying to learn more about Gladstone House. When he didn't answer I tried you. When I couldn't get you I knew something was up so I called Avery."

I frowned at her. "Wait a second. We didn't tell Avery where we were going."

Rose patted my arm somewhat condescendingly. "That child always knows what's going on. I knew if you'd come here without me it must be important. So I decided I better join you."

"It was you who rang the doorbell."

"Yes." She brushed at a wet spot on the front of her jacket. "When Annie didn't answer I knew something was wrong. I looked in the window and spotted her with the gun, herding you into that secret passage. Once the bookcase slid back into place I came inside. Honestly, who holds people at gunpoint and doesn't have the good sense to lock the front door?" She shook her head. "You know what happened after that."

I nodded. This wasn't the first time Rose had come to my rescue. My eyes suddenly filled with tears. "How many times are you going to save me?" I said, struggling to get the words out.

She smiled and took my face in her hands. "As many times as you need, sweet girl. As many times as you need."

Almost thirty-five years ago, Rose won tickets in a local radio station contest for herself and three friends to see Johnny Rock, lead singer of Johnny and the Outlaws, in concert in Camden. Rock was a talented musician with a strong singing voice who had written all of the band's original material. Back then, many people believed the Minnesota native had the potential to be a big star.

Of course Rose had invited Gram, Liz and Charlotte to go with her. Liz insisted on driving them in her big Lincoln Continental. Sadly, Rose never got to the concert. Her daughter, Abby, came down with chicken pox, and her husband was out of town. There was no way that Rose would leave Abby, not even for a few hours.

Gram offered to stay behind. So did Charlotte and Liz. Rose insisted they go to see Johnny Rock without her. In a show of solidarity, all three refused. I knew nothing about the missed concert because none of them had ever talked about it. But Rose *had* shared the story with Mr. P.

It turned out she'd had an ulterior motive for wanting to see Johnny Rock. What nobody knew was that Rose was writing songs herself back then. The concert tickets she'd won came with the opportunity to meet Johnny backstage after the show. Rose had hoped to talk to him about her writing dreams.

"Rosie put those dreams away," Mr. P. said to me. "Maybe we could give her a small part of them back."

How do you say thank you to someone who saved your life? I wasn't sure you really could.

All my life Rose had been a kind of fairy godmother. Now I had a chance to be the same for her.

Johnny Rock was back after a long time away from the stage, and sounding as good as ever. He was going to be performing at a small club in Portland. Gram, Liz and Charlotte were game for a do-over when I explained what Mr. P. and I had planned.

Mac found a place in Arundel that rented us a Lincoln Continental. It was exactly like the one Liz had owned back then except for the color. Hers had been a deep aqua. This one was a rich chocolate brown. I was driving.

Mr. P. had gotten tickets for us all to get into the club. I had no idea how he'd managed that and I didn't care. Sam, who it turned out knew Johnny, had arranged for Rose to meet the singer after the show.

"Are you sure you don't want to come with us?" I said to Mr. P. as Nick loaded everything we were taking with us into the cavernous trunk of the car.

"I'm certain," he said. "Just make sure Rosie has a good time." He raised one eyebrow. "It doesn't matter where you get your appetite, you know, as long as you eat at home." He walked over to join Nick while I tried not to picture what he meant.

Meanwhile Mac was watching me, a grin spreading across his face. "Can't say I disagree with Alfred," he said. His jacket was unzipped. I grabbed the front of his shirt, pulled him to me and kissed him hard.

"Think of that as an appetizer," I whispered.

It was time. Rose was riding shotgun. Gram, Charlotte and Liz were in the backseat. Nick tapped on the driver's side window and I rolled it down. "Call me if you have any problems," he said. "I have bail money."

"Will do," I said. I patted my sweater pocket. "I have Josh Evans on speed dial." I always had Josh on speed dial because I'd learned you never knew when you might need a lawyer.

"Let's roll, toots," Liz said.

I waved at everyone and gave Mac an extra-warm smile. Rose blew a kiss at Mr. P.

We pulled away from the curb and behind me I heard the first few notes of "I'll Be Your Home," Johnny's current release, fill the car. A moment after that all four of them were singing along and doing a pretty decent job of it.

It struck me that I was lucky. A lot luckier than Annie Hastings or Mark Steele. I was wrapped in this big blanket of love. Granted, it sometimes felt as though it would smother me, but I wouldn't trade it for anything. I knew the value of what I had.

I made the turn for the highway.

I also knew Johnny Rock—and Portland for that matter—had no idea what was coming for him.

Acknowledgments

This is the tenth Second Chance Cat Mystery. One of the reasons we've reached this milestone is because of all the booksellers who have enthusiastically recommended the series. Thank you all. Thanks as well to my editor, Jessica Wade, and my agent, Kim Lionetti, who always give their best efforts on my behalf. Thanks to Jenny Rosenstrach and her wonderful book *The Weekday Vegetarians* for inspiring my characters and me. And as always, thanks to Patrick and Lauren, who after all these years still patiently put up with my quirks.

Love Elvis the cat?
Then meet Hercules and Owen!
Read on for an excerpt from
the first book by Sofie Kelly
in the Magical Cats Mysteries . . .

CURIOSITY THRILLED THE CAT

Available in paperback
from Berkley Prime Crime!

The body was smack in the middle of my freshly scrubbed kitchen floor. Fred the Funky Chicken, minus his head.

"Owen!" I said sharply.

Nothing.

"Owen, you little fur ball, I know you did this. Where are you?"

There was a muffled "meow" from the back door. I leaned around the cupboards. Owen was sprawled on his back in front of the screen door, a neon yellow feather sticking out of his mouth. He rolled over onto his side and looked at me with the same goofy expression I used to get from stoned students coming into the BU library.

I crouched down next to the gray-and-white tabby. "Owen, you killed Fred," I said. "That's the third chicken this week."

The cat sat up slowly and stretched. He padded

over to me and put one paw on my knee. Tipping his head to one side he looked up at me with his golden eyes. I sat back against the end of the cupboard. Owen climbed onto my lap and put his two front paws on my chest. The feather was still sticking out of his mouth.

I held out my right hand. "Give me Fred's head," I said. The cat looked at me unblinkingly. "C'mon, Owen. Spit it out."

He turned his head sideways and dropped what was left of Fred the Funky Chicken's head into my hand. It was a soggy lump of cotton with that lone yellow feather stuck on the end.

"You have a problem, Owen," I told the cat. "You have a monkey on your back." I dropped what was left of the toy's head onto the floor and wiped my hand on my gray yoga pants. "Or maybe I should say you have a chicken on your back."

The cat nuzzled my chin, then laid his head against my T-shirt, closed his eyes and started to purr.

I stroked the top of his head. "That's what they all say," I told him. "You're addicted, you little fur ball, and Rebecca is your dealer."

Owen just kept on purring and ignored me. Hercules came around the corner then. "Your brother is a catnip junkie," I said to the little tuxedo cat.

Hercules climbed over my legs and sniffed the remains of Fred the Funky Chicken's head. Then he looked at Owen, rumbling like a diesel engine as I scratched the side of his head. I swear there was disdain on Hercules's furry face. Stick catnip in, on or near anything and Owen squirmed with joy. Hercules, on the other hand, was indifferent.

The stocky black-and-white cat climbed onto my lap, too. He put one white paw on my shoulder and swatted at my hair.

"Behind the ear?" I asked.

"Meow," the cat said.

I took that as a yes, and tucked the strands back behind my ear. I was used to long hair, but I'd cut mine several months ago. I was still adjusting to the change in style. At least I hadn't given in to the impulse to dye my dark brown hair blond.

"Maybe I'll ask Rebecca if she has any ideas for my hair," I said. "She's supposed to be back tonight." At the sound of Rebecca's name Owen lifted his head. He'd taken to Rebecca from the first moment he'd seen her, about two weeks after I'd brought the cats home.

Both Owen and Hercules had been feral kittens. I'd found them, or more truthfully they'd found me, about a month after I'd arrived in town. I had no idea how old they were. They were affectionate with me, but wouldn't allow anyone else to come near them, let alone touch them. That hadn't stopped Rebecca, my backyard neighbor, from trying. She'd been buying both cats little catnip toys for weeks now, but all she'd done was turn Owen into a chicken-decapitating catnip junkie. She was on vacation right now, but Owen had clearly managed to unearth a chicken from a secret stash somewhere.

I stroked the top of his head again. "Go back to sleep," I said. "You're going cold turkey . . . or maybe

I should say cold chicken. I'm telling Rebecca no more catnip toys for you. You're getting lazy."

Owen put his head down again, while Hercules used his to butt my free hand. "You want some attention, too?" I asked. I scratched the spot, almost at the top of his head, where the white fur around his mouth and up the bridge of his nose gave way to black. His green eyes narrowed to slits and he began to purr, as well. The rumbling was kind of like being in the service bay of a Volkswagen dealership.

I glanced up at the clock. "Okay, you two. Let me up. It's almost time for me to go and I have to take care of the dearly departed before I do."

I'd sold my car when I'd moved to Minnesota from Boston, and because I could walk everywhere in Mayville Heights, I still hadn't bought a new one. Since I had no car, I'd spent my first few weeks in town wandering around exploring, which is how I'd stumbled on Wisteria Hill, the abandoned Henderson estate. Everett Henderson had hired me at the library.

Owen and Hercules had peered out at me from a tumble of raspberry canes and then followed me around while I explored the overgrown English country garden behind the house. I'd seen several other full-grown cats, but they'd all disappeared as soon as I got anywhere close to them. When I left, Owen and Hercules followed me down the rutted gravel driveway. Twice I'd picked them up and carried them back to the empty house, but that didn't deter them. I looked everywhere, but I couldn't find their mother. They were so small and so determined to come with me that in the end I'd brought them home.

There were whispers around town about Wisteria Hill and the feral cats. But that didn't mean there was anything unusual about my cats. Oh no, nothing unusual at all. It didn't matter that I'd heard rumors about strange lights and ghosts. No one had lived at the estate for quite a while, but Everett refused to sell it or do anything with the property. I'd heard that he'd grown up at Wisteria Hill. Maybe that was why he didn't want to change anything.

Speaking of not wanting change, Hercules was not eager to relinquish his prime spot on my lap. But after some gentle prodding, he shook himself and got off. Owen yawned a couple of times, stretched and took twice as long to move.

I got the broom and dustpan from the porch and swept up the remains of Fred the Funky Chicken. Owen and Hercules sat in front of the refrigerator and watched. Owen made a move toward the dustpan, like he was toying with the idea of grabbing the body and making a run for it.

I glared at him. "Don't even think about it."

He sat back down, making low, grumbling meows in his throat.

I flipped open the lid of the garbage can and held the pan over the top. "Fred was a good chicken," I said solemnly. "He was a funky chicken and we'll miss him."

"Meow," Owen yowled.

I flipped what was left of the catnip toy into the garbage. "Rest in peace, Fred," I said as the lid closed.

I put the broom away, brushed the cat hair off my shirt and washed my hands. I looked in the bathroom mirror. Hercules was right. My hair did look better tucked behind my ear.

My messenger bag with a towel and canvas shoes for tai chi class was in the front closet. I set it by the door and went back through the house to make sure the cats had fresh water.

"I'm leaving," I said. But both cats had disappeared and I didn't get any answer.

I stopped to grab my keys and pick up my bag. Locking the door behind me, I headed out, down Mountain Road.

The sun was yellow-orange, low on the sky over Lake Pepin. It was a warm Minnesota evening, without the sticky humidity of Boston in late July. I shifted my bag from one shoulder to the other. I wasn't going to think about Boston. Minnesota was home now—at least for the next eighteen months or so.

The street curved in toward the center of town as I headed down the hill, and the roof of the library building came into view below. It sat on the midpoint of a curve of shoreline, protected from the water by a rock wall. The brick building had a stained-glass window that dominated one end and a copper-roofed cupola, complete with its original wrought-iron weather vane.

The Mayville Heights Free Public Library was a Carnegie library, built in 1912 with money donated by the industrialist and philanthropist Andrew Carnegie. Now it was being restored and updated to celebrate its centenary. That was why I had been in town for the last several months. And why I'd be here for the next year and a half. I was supervising the restoration—which was almost finished—as well as updating the collections, computerizing the card catalog and setting up free internet access for the library patrons. I was slowly learning the reading history of everyone in town. It made me feel like I knew the people a little, as well.

ABOUT THE AUTHOR

Sofie Ryan is a writer and mixed-media artist who loves to repurpose things in her life and in her art. She is the author of *Totally Pawstruck, Undercover Kitty,* and *Claw Enforcement* in the *New York Times* bestselling Second Chance Cat Mysteries. She also writes the *New York Times* bestselling Magical Cats Mysteries under the name Sofie Kelly.

CONNECT ONLINE

SofieRyan.com